Goods

SHORT STORIES

David Schneider

GOODS, SHORT STORIES
© 2020 David Schneider

Cuke Press DE
San Rafael, CA, and Cologne, Germany

ISBN 978-1-7363247-0-7

Illustrations by Maren März
www.marenmaerz.de
Cover and book design by Lisa Carta

Some of these stories have appeared
in edited form in *Tricycle, The Buddhist Review*

Specific places and geographies mentioned here can be identified on a map; readers may feel they recognize certain institutions. But these stories are fictional. They root themselves in the familiar, develop through invention, and flower as fiction. They are works of imagination. Many friends contributed their time, critical intelligence, and material support to this writing. It is dedicated to them, with deepest gratitude.

Contents

No Good Deed
Goes Unpublished

*I*T WASN'T A POLITICAL THING FOR ME, nor a matter of rights. I went because he asked me to, and he was a friend. Could I go over once in a while and give a talk? Just be there. Later he asked if I'd lead the morning meditation a couple of times a week. This was more tricky, not because it required a change of schedule—I was up anyway—but because it meant finding a parking place in the gay district at 4:45 a.m.

I could have walked the half hour there, but robes and sandals complicated this. Not that driving in flip-flops, or getting in and out of a car in the dark morning wearing robes, was simple. The long sleeves, the several layers of Japanese cloth, the sacred outer robe and bowing mat that were to be carried and placed respectfully, the keys, latches, and handles, the large, brimful cup of coffee. At the first stop sign one hurried morning,

I watched with dismay as my favorite cup tumbled forward from the roof of the car where I'd temporarily set it, sheeting the windshield with creamy brown liquid and smashing onto the street.

But over time I worked it out. I became the Tuesday and Thursday morning priest: the one who opened the shrines, did the morning greeting, sat there an hour and a half in meditation, and led the bowing and chanting of the morning service, before going home for breakfast. This was part of my friend's plan to get them recognition—this small cluster of gay folk who, for reasons personal and institutional, felt uncomfortable going to the main center for practice. At this point he couldn't really lead them himself—he was tied up being the Director of the main center. He'd been out most of his adult life, and though he wasn't very political, he did seem strongly motivated by a mixture of clannish pride and matronly instincts to nurture this little group.

And they were a great group: sincere in their practice and desperate, some of them, to find a patch of stability. In these early 1980s, young men dropped as though cursed by an invisible witch. AIDS had only just been identified and was not well understood; panic had begun to lace the round-the-clock-sex-party vibration of the area. So when these men, and a few women, showed up to learn or to practice meditation, they had their reasons.

Through the seasons the group grew, bought the house where some of them lived (above the basement meditation room), chose a board of directors, and became an uneasy satellite of the main center. At one point, again urged by my friend, I led a three-month practice period there, the first. It was a kind of slow-motion ordination for us all. I needed to arrive earlier each morning—no longer only twice a week—in time to ring the wake-up bell at 4:40. I gave talks, conducted private interviews, led a class, got involved in the decisions of the house—now the temple—and at the end of ninety days, sat for the combat-style Q&A ceremony. Certainly, in the course of all this we grew closer. Our lives intertwined. My respect deepened.

I don't think their being gay and lesbian influenced me much. The daily rituals of Zen—its formal greetings and constant bowing—encourage mutual respect. Practitioners are supposed to mix like milk and water. On the other hand, they were gay and lesbian; they identified that way. Society had put up significant barriers to their even existing, much less feeling OK about it, and they'd hurdled those. So when the call came, from one of the many journals sprouting out of Zen centers around the country, for an article on this group, I agreed. I felt I knew something about them—I had a constructive outlook, possibly even insights. I wrote the piece and sent it off by U.S. mail. It was accepted.

Several weeks later, I received a folded greeting card that showed a woodcut of the bodhisattva of compassion on the outside. Inside, it contained the following message:

> I am writing to you because we just found an error in your article, which will appear in Bead. Unfortunately, we did not discover it before we mailed out the issue. We send Bead by bulk mail, so it should be arriving within one to two weeks.

The error appears on page 23, second paragraph. It was typed, 'I myself am a homosexual—openly, avidly, and probably obviously so.' It should, of course, read, 'I myself am a heterosexual...'

We wish to apologize for our oversight, it's plain and simple human error. We also hope this does not cause you undue consternation. We will print a correction in our next issue which will appear about the first of next year. If you wish to respond in any way, we will also print your response. We are also open to suggestions on how you wish us to correct this error. Let us know.

Thanks again for your contribution to Bead and please accept our regrets.

Gassho...

After the signature, there was a phone number and some good times to call, several time zones away. My girlfriend's pretty blue eyes filled with tears of laughter as she read it. I think she may also have felt sympathy. We'd been living together in a flat across from the main center for a couple of years, raising a son, enjoying a social life with other couples (of all persuasions) in the neighborhood. The news that I was openly, avidly, and probably obviously homosexual might come as a shock. Lots of people read the journal. I called.

It went out bulk mail?

That's right.

And it should get to people in a week, ten days?

Something like that.

And if you were to send out a postcard with the correction on it, first class, when would that get there?

Probably around the same time, depending. It'd take us a little while to get it written, have them printed, do another mailing...

But theoretically, you could write something like what you sent me, you know—'page 23, 2nd paragraph, change homosexual to heterosexual'—and it would arrive not too much after the journal?

Yeah, I think so.

Shall we do that, then?

Sure, OK. That's a good idea. We'll do that. And again, we're so sorry.

It's all right. It happens. Good luck with the mailing.

Apparently, they got right on it, though they did it a bit differently than we'd discussed. When the postcard arrived— and it arrived several days *before* the journal—it did not focus on correcting the mistake on page 23, paragraph 2, line 6. It focused on me. It took a remorseful approach, apologizing abjectly for any possible inconvenience or misunderstanding. They wanted to make it clear to all their readership that Grady Ray was *not* a homosexual. He *was* after all a heterosexual. They were so sorry.

I found this out from my upstairs neighbor Matt. We both worked in a bakery: as the oven man, he went in to work and got home several hours before I did. This day, we passed each other in the stairwell of our building. I envied him the shower he'd clearly just had—his hair wet, pulled back into a ponytail—big in his clean T-shirt, muscular from slamming trays in and out of the rotation oven all day.

Hey, Grady, we got a postcard about you. Yeah, it said you were a heterosexual.

Man—so you know. I never had any doubts, myself.

His grin broadened.

But Arlette—Arlette was his short, curvy, flirtatious wife—Arlette was saying how good it was to get mail like that once in a while. You know, just out of the blue. A simple postcard, reminding you of your neighbor's sexual orientation. Just in case, you know, it might slip your mind.

The Dress

RADY SAW THE DRESS SHORTLY AFTER 11:00 AM, on a December day toward the end of 1984. It hung on a headless mannequin in a room he was shown as part of an apartment tour. He'd arrived at 11:00, lugged his bodywork table up thirty stairs and at the top met Troy, who had AIDS. Troy waited back a bit from the top of the stairs, so Grady hadn't seen him till he got to the top.

They toured around the apartment, sizing each other up. Troy wasn't hard to size up: he was in terrible shape—6'2", as white himself as the long nightshirt he wore, and rail thin. He was recovering from a bout of pneumonia, and his lover, Jules, had arranged for Grady to come to the house to see if perhaps bodywork would speed his recovery, or at least make him more comfortable.

As he showed Grady around, Troy took credit for the tasteful and obviously expensive decor. In a room that Jules used for meditation, Grady saw the dress. It was black from the waist to a strapless top, with a full black and gold skirt falling to the ankle; various kinds of silk and raw silk, flawlessly sewn. The dress clung to the top of the mannequin, then flared away at the hips.

Troy noticed Grady's interest and said he'd designed it himself and had it sewn. Grady couldn't resist a comment about the figure beneath the dress. Troy brightened. You ought to see the girl who models for me.—you'd love her.

Yeah?

She's very exotic. She's got this white-white skin and jet black hair.

Grady eyed the mannequin again: trim waist, breast, lovely hips.

You designed it just for her?

Well, this one is a sample. But yes, I made it to fit Lisa. Usually I design for, like, the matrons of Pacific Heights. I'll get about $2,000 for one of these dresses. You know, they have to have something nobody else has for opening night at the opera or something.

Right.

And Lisa, she's great. I have lots of ideas for these samples and I love to work with her— An ugly coughing cut his sentence short.

They found a warm room, and Grady unpacked his table and started to massage Troy. Grady had to work very gently, very deliberately; soon Troy was alternating between sleepy periods and gossipy good moods. During a talkative spurt, the conversation edged back toward Lisa.

Oh, Troy clucked, She works as a manicurist downtown. I'll give you the number. For twelve dollars she'll hold your hand for an hour.

Grady actually thought it over. He'd been wanting a manicure for a while—a crazy idea about how doing bodywork for a living meant his money came from work with his hands, and how smart it would be to pamper them more and take good care of them.

They finished the session, and having enjoyed each other sufficiently, scheduled another. Grady left, forgetting until he was in his car to ask for Lisa's phone number.

A week later, Grady was back at Troy's, and thought he looked better. There was color in his cheeks and a somewhat sturdier feel to him. In the middle of the session, Grady wandered down the long, narrow, thickly carpeted hall to the bathroom. On the way back, he peeked into the room that housed the dress. It was still there, elegant and sexy.

Gently working on the back of Troy's legs, he pressed forward with questions about Lisa.

You remember that manicurist who models for you? You were going to tell me how to go hold hands with her.

Lisa? Sure, she works at Rakes, on Bush Street downtown. I used to go there myself when Yvette was doing pedicure. See, Yvette was this Hungarian lady—she was incredible. She was like this psychic. I mean, you'd go to get your feet done, but meanwhile this woman was an incredible *healer* or something. So this clientele grew up around her...

Troy went on for many minutes, telling Grady the entire history of the salon, particularly how he met Jules there. His story included a detailed account of the fractious politics, which eventually led to a schism. Several of the girls had bolted to start their own place. While Lisa had remained at Rakes, Troy now patronized the new place, where the pedicurist had gone, so he didn't see Lisa nearly as much as he had. He did see her for modeling, and was close enough with her, he thought, that she'd tell him if she stopped working at Rakes. Most likely she was still there.

A few days later Grady found himself downtown, in the vague vicinity of Rakes. Having finished his errands, he walked up Bush for more blocks than he'd guessed before he came to the proper address. It turned out to be a sort of miniature mall: stores and boutiques crammed together on three levels behind a facade of iron girders painted cranberry. A security guard in a cranberry coat watched as he went down to the basement level, where, according to the directory, he'd find Rakes.

At the bottom, he clutched the brass bannister and thought of turning back. This is madness, vanity, lechery. I'm the only male down here, the clothes on the women waiting in there look a lot more expensive than my clothes. I feel shabby. Vanity and lechery.... He went in.

He walked to the appointment desk, and asked the dark-haired woman there for an appointment with Lisa.

And when would you like to come, sir?

When's good?

Well, Lisa could see you next Friday, at 2:45—is that OK?

Fine. How long does this take? Nothing sooner?

No, sir, that's her first opening. You want it? Appointments are for one hour.

Sure, sure. Write me down.

She did, and gave Grady a card which had printed on it the Rakes name, logo, address, and phone. Below that she had written Lisa—Friday, January 23, 2:45 p.m.

See you next week, and be sure to call twenty-four hours ahead if you need to cancel.

Grady climbed back up to the damp January air on Bush St., feeling brave, foolish, vain, and lecherous. He was also now running late.

Friday the 23rd he worried inordinately long about what to wear, finally deciding on some black wool pants, a white shirt, and a red jacket. His shoes looked a little beat up, but it was too late to do anything about them. Grady finished a bodywork session at 2:15, bought a sandwich in a corner grocery, and ate it while driving downtown. Friday afternoon parking was ridiculous but he found a space a block and a half from Rakes. He breezed in about three minutes late and was told to take a seat.

While he waited, he looked at the Italian *Vogue* and exchanged furtive glances with the women waiting. His stylist, he was told, would come get him when she was ready. Ten minutes gone on the meter.

Finally, someone said, Grady? He looked up from Giannini Versace's models on a beach in *Vogue* to a replica of a Giannini Versace model standing in front of him. One foot pointed toward Grady—the other, at 90 degrees to the first, pointed down the hall. The feet were encased in wide, patent leather shoes, and the weight of the body was on the back hip, the one with the foot pointing down the hall.

That's me.

Come on. This way.

Grady followed her down the hall. He hadn't yet had a good look at her face, but from behind she looked great. Her straight, jet-black hair hung to mid-back and bounced from side to side as she walked. She wore a tight, dark-green corduroy jumpsuit. He could see that she had good legs and walked with an enthusiastic lateral movement in each stride. Her upper body moved all as a piece, somewhat stiffly, and her shoulders were wide and thin. When she turned and motioned Grady ahead of her into the manicure room, he noticed that she led with her pelvis, in a kind of slouch. He also saw that she was indeed as pale as composition paper.

Grady sat down in a chair behind a little table, trying not to move awkwardly, though he felt that Lisa, the other three manicurists, and their clients were all watching closely as he squeezed into his seat. He had to use the same movements a high-schooler would use getting seated at a second grader's desk. Lisa pulled her chair directly in front of him and they sat with knees almost touching, faces about two feet apart, a metal tray-table between them, on which were the tools of her trade.

Soak your hands in this for a few minutes, she said.

Her figure looked good from the front too: narrow waist, high, separate, not-large breasts, and a long neck. Lisa's eyes were wide and dark, set far apart in her face. She had a long, straight nose, high cheekbones, and black bangs. Her mouth was also wide, lips neither thick nor thin.

Lisa grabbed his left hand in both of hers and pulled it toward her. She curled forward until her eyes were almost on top of his nails. He suddenly felt embarrassed about them: the nails were clipped short—a grooming necessity for a bodyworker. *Maybe there won't be anything for her to do other than asking me why I even came in here*, he thought.

Lisa looked up at Grady, then back to his nails. These look *terrible*, she announced. Don't you ever do your cuticles?

I guess not.

And how come your nails are so short? Never mind.

I'm a bodyworker. I do bodywork for a living.

What?

I work on people's bodies for money. Just like you do, he said, lowering his volume as he spoke. The other women in the room were looking at them. The one next to Grady craned her neck to see what was so terrible about his nails.

Hmm, said Lisa, reaching for an emery board. She began pushing the cuticles of his left hand up toward his wrist. She crossed her legs and bent further forward. It looked uncomfortable, and Grady said so. Lisa replied that she did ache at the end of a day, and then, more playfully, she suggested she come see him for bodywork. He said maybe, and gave her one of his cards.

So how come you have a shaved head? she blurted. Is it all right to ask you that? I wasn't sure, but I couldn't help myself.

It's fine. I shave my head because I'm a Zen priest.

Oh, Lisa said, in two separate tones, the second lower than the first. What's that like?

Grady laughed. He didn't know how to answer the question; he also guessed he couldn't get away with a chuckle. As if to confirm his guess, her gaze flashed up from his hand to his eyes. He felt the same way he had when she first stared up from his neglected cuticles—pinned, exposed.

Well, it's great, sort of, he said. I mean, I like it a lot. I don't know how anyone else—

Do you take vows? You know, poverty, chastity, that stuff? I was raised Catholic. Does everyone have to shave their head? She swooped down again to his nails.

No, you don't have to shave your head or anything—only if you want to be ordained. If you're ordained, you're supposed to keep your head shaved, and you take vows. But they're not—I mean, I could have a job, get married, have a girlfriend or something.

Hmm, she hummed. Grady went on talking immediately, rather than risk another immobilizing glance. You are supposed to do these things, he continued, if you end up doing them, in sort of an exemplary way—you know?

Mmm-hmm, but what do you do?

Me? Oh, I'm exemplary, he replied.

She smiled and Grady smiled back.

Listen, I'm parked at a meter....

You want to run now and come right back? Lisa looked up and sat back in her chair.

Sure, I'll be right back.

The cold air of the street snapped Grady out of what felt like a spell. He jogged to the car with a distinct feeling that he was taking time out from something other than a manicure. When he returned, somewhat breathless, Lisa was not there. He sat down and looked around. Two of the other customers seemed to know each other and were engaged in conversation. A third woman wearing a gray suit and white silk shirt looked as if she was simply enduring her manicure. Over the sound system he heard *When a*

Man Loves a Woman. Lisa strolled back into the room, snapping her fingers lazily, and humming. I love this song, don't you?

Yeah, I do.

Who did this? Isn't it, um, Otis Redding?

No, I think it's Percy Sledge.

Really? Can't be. Gloria? Lisa swiveled in her seat to address the manicurist behind her. Isn't this Otis Redding? Or is it Percy Sledge? Both Gloria and her client looked at Grady and said they thought it was Percy Sledge too.

You like soul music, then? Lisa asked, and before he could reply, she added, I love it.

Yeah, I love it too—anyway, I used to. I was a really big fan in the 60s. I used to go see the Temptations every time they came to town. I even have Eddie Kendricks's and Davie Ruffin's autographs.

This seemed to impress her more than anything Grady had said so far. They fell to talking about music of the 60s and 70s and their respective preferences.

They had little in common: she liked rap. What he'd heard of it sounded repetitive. She frequented the after-hours scene. He habitually got up at 4:00 a.m. to drink coffee and otherwise prepare for meditation, and so was completely unfamiliar with nightlife.

How old are you? she asked suddenly, waiting for his answer with her emery board poised above his fingers.

How old do I look?

She inspected his face very closely. It's hard to tell with no hair, but, I don't know, thirty?

Thirty-four. And you?

How old do I look?

I should have known you'd say that. What, twenty-four?

Twenty-six. Pretty good.

At the end of the manicure, he thanked her and walked to the front desk to pay. Troy had told Grady how it was done. You paid $12, and left $3 for your manicurist at the front desk. Lisa followed Grady up, and while he was paying, she stepped into a small room by the desk, which Grady assumed was the staff restroom. She came out a minute later and handed him a little slip of paper. On it, in red pen, she had written her full name, , and her work and home phone numbers. He looked up from the paper. She looked at him and said, Call me.

Early evening, Grady began looking for a date. He felt it was too soon to call Lisa, so he called Ann. They were good friends, hot for each other, but Ann lived with someone. Her boyfriend didn't always treat her very well, and when things got unendurable, she'd go see Grady for a movie, or dinner, and some harmless making out. Afterward, she seemed to feel better about everything. She'd get back into one or another of her new cars (her boyfriend was very wealthy) and go home. The boyfriend was in Colorado skiing now, and Ann and Grady were making plans to rendezvous when he heard clicks on his line, signaling another call. He excused himself to Ann, who was gracious about it, and took the call.

Hello?

Hi.

He waited, but the caller offered no further identification. Grady sometimes enjoyed succeeding at this test but found the game considerably more difficult for being in the middle of a conversation. Finally he recognized the voice as Lisa's—a sandy, low-pitched sound which could glide high instantly higher.

Lisa?

Yeah.

Let me call you right back, I'm on the other line.

He told Ann excitedly that *the manicurist* had called. As a friend, she took an active interest in what she termed his other girls. She knew about today's visit to the manicurist, and teased him lightly before wishing him luck and hanging up.

Grady got right back to Lisa. She answered the phone with Hi. After they finished asking each other how the rest of the day had gone, she asked, Are you busy now? Tonight?

Ann flitted briefly through his mind as he said no.

So, do you want to go see that movie we talked about?

Which one was that?

You know, the Bette Midler one.

Sure—OK, he lied. There were lots of movies he did want to see, but the Bette Midler was not one of them.

Well, it's playing right near my house. Why don't you come over around nine, and we'll go to the late show.

Fine, he heard himself say, knowing he was due up at 4:00. She gave him the address, some hints about parking, and hung up.

Two hours later, he set out. She lived on Bush near Polk—not quite the Tenderloin, not quite dangerous, but not far from it. Grady parked and rang her bell. An older, short, plump gay man and his young friend walked past him and let themselves in, but Grady waited outside for Lisa. Peering in through the grimy glass of the front door, he saw her come down. First her feet, in black spike heels against the worn green floral carpet of the stairs, then her legs, covered in black tights. Next came a short, tight, black leather skirt, and then what looked like the top of a camisole, also black. She smiled saucily as she opened the front door.

You look terrific, he said.

Really? Thanks. Come in, please, I'm not quite ready—do you mind?

Not at all.

He followed her again, happily. They climbed the stairs to the third floor.

My apartment's a mess, she said.

It was true. A short hallway by the door housed a dresser: both hall and dresser were strewn with clothes. The main room, the studio—with kitchen attached—was equally littered. Broccoli sat in a steamer on a dirty stove. Days of dishes filled the sink. Books, magazines, and bottles cluttered the kitchen table; a battered old phone and answering machine were crammed onto another small table. The room smelled like broccoli.

Only the area by her bed seemed at all tidy. The bed itself, which was on the floor, was neatly made and covered with a zebra hide. Two long columnar pillows rested on the hide against the wall. A low bedside table held an orderly array of cremes and lotions, and at the foot of the bed, on a cabinet, her television broadcast a picture but no sound.

Grady sat down on the only chair in her place, and moved the answering machine so he could rest his arm on the table. Lisa grabbed a sprig of broccoli and bit off the top.

You hungry? she asked

No thanks.

Sorry I'm late, I got talking to a girlfriend on the phone.

It's all right.

They talked a bit, then noticed it was getting late. Lisa grabbed the steamer with broccoli in it and balanced it on the pile in the sink. She began darting around the apartment, picking things up, straightening, consolidating. She slung her leather jacket over one shoulder, then stopped abruptly.

Do you really want to go to this movie?

Not really. No. Do you?

Huh-uh.

Well, what do you want to do, then?

I'd like to just stay here and watch my favorite TV programs. There's this incredible yoga lady—have you ever seen her?

I can't say I have.

Well, she's so cute—she's got this Southern accent. She's kind of fat, or plump, really....

Grady stopped listening to her and began to consider his luck.

After they watched yoga, Lisa ran through the channels. It occurred to Grady that he would have to advance matters, or he'd drown in television. She had joined him on the zebra skin, and was sitting in front of him. Grady put one hand on the back of her shoulder and one on her waist, and pulled her gently back. He leaned forward and whispered in her long, cool black hair, Would you like to kiss?

She turned to face him and said nothing. She just looked in his eyes.

You don't want to kiss?

I didn't say that, she said. She moved her head toward him extremely slowly and held his eyes with her gaze. Her approach seemed theatrical, and Grady felt for a second that he was in a movie. She didn't bother to pucker her lips, or shape them in any way he could match. She simply laid them slowly, gently, and slightly parted on his, and held them there for a few seconds. While their lips were touching and they could get no closer, it felt to Grady that she was still coming toward him. She then pulled back, as slowly as she had come in, looking at him.

He'd never been kissed like that before, and didn't quite know what to make of it. He did know he wanted more. At the same time, he could see how much she enjoyed running things. He reclined, stared at her, and let her come back to him, which she did. This time she opened her mouth and they began a lazy French kissing. She kissed creatively, sucking his tongue into her mouth. He trapped her lower lip, tongued it, and bit it softly. They both began to breathe very deeply when she suddenly closed off the kiss and pulled back.

What's that on your tongue? she asked.

What?

What's on the tip of your tongue?

Nothing. Grady got up, crossed the room to the full-length mirror on her closet door, and examined his tongue. True enough, on the very tip was an extremely small white bump.

You're right—there's this teeny little bump.

I don't mind, I just wondered. Come back here.

Grady went back, impressed with the sensitivity of her tongue. He settled down and began to kiss her again. He loved to kiss—it was his favorite part. Grady had observed that if a woman kissed well, she would usually turn out to be sexually skilled. On the other hand, just because someone didn't kiss the way he liked, she might be masterful in one of the more advanced acts. But Lisa could certainly kiss, and as they rocked against each other on the bed, Grady felt that she also possessed extraordinary control of her hips.

Grady worked a hand under her black camisole and her black lace bra and found a breast that filled his hand. Lisa continued kissing him for a while, without removing his hand. Then she pulled back, tugged his shirt out of his pants and started to unbutton it. Grady let her. He watched as she kneeled over him and carefully undid all the buttons. He hadn't taken his hand out of her bra, so his arm was suspended in air, with his wrist at an awkward angle, but he didn't mind. He finally relinquished his hold and wriggled out of both his shirt and undershirt.

Lisa looked him over slowly as she pushed down the straps of her camisole. She pulled it over her head, and then one at a time pushed down the straps of her bra. Reaching behind her, she unhooked the bra and threw it on the floor. Holding Grady's eyes with her own, she lay down on top of him and began to kiss him, slowly at first and then more passionately, fueled by skin contact. She tossed her head to the side from time to time, to pull a long stray hair from between their tongues. She stared at him briefly and grinned each time before kissing him more.

Grady hardened beneath his pants and pressed himself against her leg. Lisa seemed in no hurry to remove his pants. Now that she had him half naked on her bed, half naked herself, she seemed content to just kiss and writhe on him. Grady too felt content; he was mesmerized by Lisa's staring and kissing.

He hadn't really expected to get this far with her, and was in no mood to jeopardize his gains by being pushy. This seemed to be her show, and going along with it seemed to be the right tack. It had been a good show so far. He felt a little unsure—anything might or might not happen.

Lisa suddenly stood up from the low bed. I'm going to put some music on, she said. Watching her walk across the room topless, in high heels, tights, and a leather skirt made Grady very happy. She put on some hip group—sad, pleasant, unobtrusive— and walked back across the room toward him.

Soon she was out of her shoes, skirt, and tights. Grady also got down to his underpants. They kissed incessantly as they pulled themselves and each other out of clothes. From time to time, Lisa backed away to do something necessary—she'd walk across the room to change the tape, adjust a light, pull a window closed. Grady reveled, watching her walk around in her panties. Lisa obviously enjoyed displaying her body for him. After she ran out of things to do to the environment, she began to model dresses. She modeled those she owned and those that were still being designed, soliciting his opinion about them, but not really paying much attention to what he said.

Grady got up to pee. He shuffled over to Lisa—momentarily between dresses—and kissed her. They stood in the middle of the room topless, kissing, swaying to the music now coming from the blaster. They began to move their tongues and hips together in rhythm with the bass—a rolling, syncopated figure. They ground against each other, dancing at the same time. They were touching their mouths, tongues, shoulders, forearms and hands, waists, hip bones, pelvises, knees, and toes. They moved as one thing, and as they did, Grady noticed that the angle of her pubic bone was somehow different, a little flatter maybe, than he was used to.

He broke the kiss this time.

I really have got to go pee. Between you and having to pee, I'm about swollen out the top of these pants.

Lisa looked down, reached a forefinger inside his underpants, and pulled the elastic toward her. Grady's dick stood there, quite at attention.

Hmmm, she said. She looked at it a while, looked at Grady, then gently let the elastic go, patted him through his underpants, and said, Go pee.

In her small, dim bathroom, cluttered with cosmetics, Grady watched himself. Lisa had a mirror on top of the toilet. Though he had seen this arrangement in the bathrooms of many women he knew in San Francisco, he'd never really understood it. This time, he noticed he wore a silly grin.

He finished and went back into the main room of the apartment, which Lisa had now darkened. Only a small bedside lamp shone—behind it he saw Lisa in bed. Grady pulled back the zebra hide and got in next to her. As they kissed, Grady felt the weight of the entire day descend on him. Despite an obvious state of arousal, he yawned.

Lisa chuckled. I'm tired too—why don't we just go to sleep? There's no big hurry, is there?

No, you're right, Grady said, and curled on his side behind her. He put his arms around her and she molded her body to his. Her back lay against his chest, her legs jumbled with his, and her rear nestled comfortably into his crotch. Grady fell asleep with a hand between Lisa's breasts.

A light sleep covered them like smoke around a cigarette. Grady slept fitfully for being in a strange bed; Lisa seemed to sleep the same way for having a visitor in hers. Three hours later, the electric alarm he'd set barked at an unbelieving Grady. He finally made it to his feet, splashed water in his eyes, kissed Lisa goodbye, and went out to find his car.

At 5:00 a.m., as he began the first period of meditation, Grady felt warm and still distinctly aroused from the night before. But midway through the second period, the effects of his hot shower and coffee wore off; he fought drowsiness ineffectually and fell, chilled, into a self-critical snooze.

Over the next few weeks Grady and Lisa dated several times; they usually met for dinner. Grady would be winding his day down; Lisa would be getting into gear for her long evenings at the clubs, yet they managed to bring a lively attention to each other at dinner.

On their first date, at Grady's suggestion, they ate in a small noodle shop in Japantown. When they walked in together, the mostly Japanese clientele stopped eating and stared at them. Take my coat! Lisa mouthed at him, and Grady practically swept the long, leather jacket from her. Feeling like a good spectacle, they sat down. When dinner arrived, they ate heavily. Grady was surprised at first by how much and how quickly she ate, but he concluded that dinner must be her only real meal of the day. They talked rapidly; a hidden music seemed to inform their conversation—a steady, pushy beat.

Lisa slowed only when they began to discuss family backgrounds. She poked at the remains of her noodles, had several sips of beer, and told Grady she was part Chinese, part Mexican, and that her parents lived somewhere down the Peninsula. Grady burbled through his third beer that he couldn't care less about anyone's ethnic background unless he was driving behind them, which made Lisa laugh. She inhaled the rest of her food, what was left of both their beers, and clucked at Grady to hurry up.

From then on, they ate only in Chinese or Mexican restaurants, special ones that Lisa knew. Grady would pick her up at work, or meet her at a bar. They'd ferret out a little-known pot sticker place or taqueria, drink a string of beers, and eat to satiety. During the meals, Lisa often grabbed one of Grady's hands and began remedial cuticle work.

The arrangements for future meetings were casual:

Call me tomorrow?

No, you call me.

OK, what time?

Whenever. If I don't hear from you by about two, I'll call you.

Thursday, as Grady swerved out of the fast one-way traffic in front of Lisa's building, he saw her slouched on the stoop, smoking a cigarette, long legs stretched out in front of her. She recognized his car, stubbed out her smoke, smoothed her long, leather skirt, and smiled. She got in his car and kissed him. Grady tasted the tobacco on her breath and found it delicious. He'd often wished he could smoke himself, but having given it up once, he hadn't dared to start again.

On the ride to one of Lisa's taquerias, she chatted breathily about her day and bounced a small, hard rubber ball against the inside of his windshield.

Stop that, would you? he asked her.

Lisa smiled and said, No, I don't think I will.

After dinner they walked to his car, which Grady had parked in the lot of the adjacent funeral parlor. Lisa pulled the ball from the pocket of her coat and began to bounce it against the brick wall of the funeral parlor. She laughed wildly as the ball bounced off the hoods and windows of the other cars in the lot. The bangles on her wrists clanked against one another as she lurched to corral the crazily bouncing ball. Grady wondered what it sounded like to the patrons of the parlor, if there were any that night. He gallantly got to his knees and fetched the ball from beneath a Corvette as Lisa, slightly drunk, leaned against the adjacent car and laughed.

Grady opened the passenger door, kissed Lisa, and pushed her into the front seat without giving her the ball. Get in, and be a little quiet, would you?

No, I don't think I will, Lisa replied, leaning back in the seat, arranging her hair over the headrest, switching on the radio, and closing her eyes. No, I won't. Grady drove to his apartment as Lisa crooned along with the radio, popped her fingers, and let the wind from her rolled-down window blow through her hair.

At Grady's little duplex, he unlocked the metal gate, then the inside door, and ushered Lisa upstairs. He opened the refrigerator and pulled out some beers. Lisa stood at the door of his too-bright kitchen, squinting. He handed her a beer, and nudged her out of the room, into the hallway. About three steps toward his room, he pressed his body against hers, pressed her against the wall, and began kissing her. She kissed him back hotly.

He began to move her slowly against the wall, his beer bottle held in a hand around her waist, clunking loudly against the wall with each pulse. She wrapped a leg around his waist, and again they began to move together, tongues and pelvises locked. He dropped his bottle on the floor, and they giggled into each other's mouths as the beer fizzed slowly out onto the rug by their feet. With his hand free, Grady began to knead Lisa's lower back. He clutched her skin and worked his hand inside her skirt and panties. It was tight, but he slipped his middle finger straight down and let his other fingers luxuriate in the flesh of her cheeks. Lisa unwrapped her leg and edged Grady down the hallway, never breaking her kiss.

In Grady's room, Lisa pushed him away for a moment to catch her breath.

I'll see you in just a second, Grady said, and went back up the hall to collect the beer bottle. He made a quick stop in the bathroom, feeling very sure of himself.

When he got back to his room, Lisa was looking at one of his books. She folded it onto his desk, and embraced him again. This time Grady slid both his hands down her hips and let them rest on the back of her legs. They kissed again and he pulled her skirt slowly up, hand over hand, until finally his hands were on the stockings at the very top of her legs, just below her rear. He ran his fingers along the crevices there, pulling outward, opening her from behind. Suddenly Lisa took a quick gasping breath and worked her arms up inside his embrace. She laid her fists against his chest and pushed him far enough away for conversation.

Have you talked to Troy since we've been going out? Did he say anything to you?

Yeah, sure, I talked to him. He wants to know everything all the time. He grills me.

Grady tried to move back in for a wet kiss, and Lisa let him, but coolly. He kissed away at her for a second, then stopped.

Is there something he should have said to me? he asked, unlocking his fingers from her rear end and relocking them around her waist.

Oh, she said, two-toned. No, I don't think so.

Lisa, is there something you're not telling me?

Not telling you? she said, with an uncontrollable grin.

Please don't do this—don't play this kind of game.

I'm not playing any games with you, idiot, she replied, banging her fists against his chest. She shoved him again with her fists, and he tripped on his low mattress. As Grady fell, he caught her wrists and pulled Lisa down with him onto the mattress. She fell on him heavily, and then bounced up onto her knees and tried to pin him. Grady worked to flip her over, but she had his shoulders under her knees and she was laughing wildly.

Lisa, Grady said, I'm telling you...

Telling me what, big boy?

Telling you... From flat on his back, Grady hoisted his legs up till his ankles wrapped around her shoulders. He tried to pull her back off him with his ankles, but they were both giggling so hard he found it difficult to muster the strength. Finally, with a samurai shout and a slight fart, Grady succeeded. Lisa fell back with a shriek, and in a second their positions were reversed: Grady pinned Lisa's shoulders to the mattress with his hands, and looked into her eyes.

I know, he gasped, In your deep, dark secret past, you were a man.

He had no idea why he said it, but the minute he did, he feared it was true. He'd never actually thought it; the words just slipped out of his mouth without consideration.

Lisa's eyes widened, then returned to normal. No, she said.

Thank god, Grady said mentally.

But I was a boy.

What?

I was a boy.

What do you mean?

I mean I had a sex-change operation.

There was a long pause. Grady continued looking in her eyes, but her face had begun changing. He looked more. Finally, he said, You're kidding.

Lisa just looked back at him.

When did this happen?

I was completed last year.

COMPLETED? Grady's mind screamed at him, COMPLETED?

Is this freaking you out? Lisa asked.

No... No, tell me about it. He released Lisa's shoulders from their pinned position and lay down beside her, propping himself on an elbow, where he could see her. It was amazing. Her face had completely ceased being female, and Grady could not get it to look that way again. Look and look again, and all he got was a sweet, young Mexican boy with long hair. He felt as if he were looking at an optical illusion that had switched from one image to its trick reverse. He had lost the key to the first image. He noticed, somewhat uncomfortably, that his dick hadn't received any confusing messages yet. It was still raring.

For the next hour Lisa told him pretty exactly what was required of a person who wanted to change sexes. She described how she had gone through it: the long chain of psychiatric interviews—a year at least—and the year of cross-dressing, the series of operations, how her family had been supportive and had helped her recover.

Grady felt many things as he listened. At times he held her close to him. At times he tuned out the words and just stared. He wondered who this person was; he felt she was one of the most courageous people he'd met. Equally clear to him was that at core, she was female. But he couldn't get her to look like one again. He saw stages between male and female as she described them, but Lisa never returned to looking female.

When you were a boy, did you ever have sex with a woman?

Yeah. Once. I tried it, but it didn't do that much for me.

How about with guys?

Um-hmm. I did that too, but not very often. I was pretty scared of the whole thing, you know.

Grady thought for a while. Since your operations, have you been with a guy?

Oh yeah. I had one boyfriend for quite a while, a Danish guy. And then I've dated some.

Did they know?

Sure, I had to tell them.

Were they OK with it?

Some were, some weren't. The Danish guy liked it. He liked me, I guess.

I like you too, Lisa.

You do, still? You're sweet. Are you still interested in sex?

Sure, Grady said before he could give himself a chance to think.

Because if you are, it's going to take a little preparation.

What do you mean?

Well, I can't just do it without preparation, unless the guy is really small, which you aren't. I checked.

What do you mean by preparation?

If you've had a sex change, and if you aren't being sexually active, then you tend to close up a little. You close up, and you can't take anything sizeable in there. So I have to wear something for a few days. I have to wear a kind of dildo, to open me back up.

Grady was stunned. Well, start wearing it then, would you?

OK Lisa replied, seeming pleased.

By this point, Grady's head was a sweetish mixture of admiration and compassion, his guts felt slightly uneasy, but his dick was happily, ignorantly hard.

Well, there are other things we could do, he suggested, for right now.

What are you thinking of?

You know—head, and all that.

Oh. I don't really like that. I'm just not into sucking dick, if you know what I mean.

Crestfallen, Grady continued. I understand—I'm not either. What do you like, then?

Well, I like anal sex.

Oh, my goodness, Grady thought. Warning bells were going off in his head: *I don't know this girl, really, except for this wild story, and I know she's been with guys, and I'm no expert at anal sex, and there must be, like, tricks or techniques or something... Oh, god.*

Lisa read some of this in his face and said, It's OK, sweetie. There's no hurry, is there?

No, I guess not.

There is one other thing, though, Lisa said.

What's that?

When they were finishing me up, the doctor gave me a choice. He said I could look sort of more normal down there, and feel less, or I could feel quite a bit more, but I'd look a little abnormal.

Which did you choose?

I chose to feel more.

That's what I would have done too, probably, Grady said. How abnormal is it?

Here, Lisa said, Give me your hand. She took Grady's hand in her own, and pushed it beneath her skirt, into her panties. He felt around. It felt good to him, not very unusual. Long lips, sensitive, as he could tell from the change in Lisa's breathing. He liked it, and he began to harden again, out of his alarmed and wilted state.

It's getting kind of late, sweetie, isn't it? Lisa asked suddenly. I mean, we've both been through quite a bit tonight. I don't want to keep you up, so to speak. Why don't you just take me home now, and we'll continue all this later, OK?

Yeah. OK, that's fine, Grady said, with the most thorough mix of relief and disappointment he could ever remember feeling. Fine.

Next morning in meditation, sweetness had gone from his head, and no energy filled his groin. All he felt was a gnawing, widening uneasiness in the middle of his body.

He saw Troy for a session of bodywork later in the day. Troy appeared to be holding his own pretty well against the virus, but Grady was not in a congratulatory mood. Very funny, guys, he snapped at Troy and Jules as he unpacked his table. Why didn't you tell me?

Listen to him, Troy said to Jules. Tell you what?

About Lisa.

What about Lisa?

You know—her operations and all.

What operations? What are you talking about?

About her sex-change, god damn it.

Oh get out of here. You don't believe that, do you?

Don't you?

We heard some rumor a long time ago, but we never took it seriously.

Well, believe it.

You are kidding.

That's what I said to her. I wish I were, but I'm not. No, she used to be a boy. Now she's a girl.

That is so far out, that is just really wild, Troy said. He seemed delighted. Are you still going out with her?

I did last night. I guess I still will.

Well, let us know how everything goes. We want to know every detail.

Yeah, yeah. Now hush up and take off your clothes and lie down on the table.

Yes sir, Mr. Man. Right away.

It fell apart quickly. Little ways Grady and Lisa had clicked now became ways they missed. *No sir, she's not in right now—can I take a message?* A recorder instead of a voice. A busy tone. The invisible thread that strung them so loosely together had been severed. A delayed call, clicks on the line instead of a message.

One wet evening several weeks later, Grady came in from

working in a chiropractic office. He'd fought traffic in the dark rain for more than an hour to get home. There was a message from Lisa on his machine, in a meek and formal voice:

Hi Grady, this is Lisa Gutierrez calling—I hope you are well. I'm doing very well myself... There's no message, really... Tell Troy and Jules hello for me... I just called to wish you a very happy Easter.

The Next Big Thing

THE DIRECTOR CALLED ME RIGHT AWAY, MIDMORNING. He has a sign on his desk that glares at the reader—DO IT TODAY—so no sooner had the call come in than he was in my ear. He'd been contacted by the city's Mortuary Office: the woman there was looking for a Buddhist funeral, and she'd landed on us. Could we do one? He knew and I knew that we could, but it depended. There were always circumstances.

When the Mortuary lady called me, she sounded relieved to be making a little progress, though in explaining the situation, she had a hard time saying the Asian names. She'd heard from a Chinese man. She struggled with his name, and with our group's name, which is based on Sanskrit. While not as difficult as Chinese, it does combine letters in a way unfamiliar to Germans.

Soon I was speaking with Mr. Xiao himself—he pronounced his name with at least two syllables, and these at distinct pitches. I'd never heard anything quite like it. He explained his situation in bits and pieces, and at the same time he interviewed me, rather suspiciously. Was I Buddhist? Could I perform a funeral? He had my name from the City.

I answered him and tried to establish facts. When did he imagine the funeral taking place?

Next week. In a few days. Tuesday?

I said I'd have to get back to him.

We snagged on the ceremony. Our group descends from a Tibetan lineage, and our ceremony had been composed by a Tibetan master. He told me that he was Han Chinese. Then, almost as if confiding a secret, he let me know that they regarded Tibet as part of China. Where he came from, there were many more Chinese than Tibetans.

Well, that's the only ceremony I have for you, I said. Mr.—.

He intoned his name again. It sounded to me like a doorbell. Or a cat.

I suggested he visit our centre first and look at the space. The Director could give him a tour, and he could see if it made sense to talk further. He agreed to this plan, and after an exchange of coordinates, we hung up. I felt sure I'd never hear from him again. But that afternoon, the Director called to say that Mr. Xiao had indeed come by, and wanted to proceed. Mr. Xiao was apparently nice enough, though the situation sounded strange. The Director wasn't quite sure who the funeral was actually for. Perhaps there'd been a misunderstanding? Anyway, could I please take this on? Mr. Xiao wanted it on Tuesday midday.

I pointed out that Tuesday midday there would be trouble rounding up a crowd, and that in my experience Chinese funerals were supposed to be big: banks of flowers, clouds of incense, heavy costumes, long recitations, music, a large gathering, wailing, if possible. The Director said he would see what he could do and hung up.

When we next spoke, Mr. Xiao immediately rehearsed the geopolitics: he was Han Chinese; there weren't many Tibetans in his part of China; Tibet belonged to China, anyway. When he finished I asked him for whom we were doing the funeral.

His wife's father.

Would his wife be coming to the funeral?

No, she was in China.

Where was the father?

He was here, in cold storage. He'd been brought here for the funeral.

How long had he been here?

About a month. It had taken Mr. Xiao a while to find us.

Why was the father here?

The father had been Buddhist. The daughter was Buddhist. They wanted a Buddhist funeral.

And?

And they weren't allowed to do a Buddhist funeral in his part of China.

Hmm.

So she'd packed the father up and sent him here, where he—Mr. Xiao—was in school. Because you *could* do a Buddhist funeral in Germany.

I told him that Tuesday morning we would prepare the room and the shrine, and right before the ceremony, the transport people could bring the body up and put it in the shrine room. We would do the ceremony. It would last about a half hour. I couldn't guarantee that there'd be many people, Tuesday being a workday, and today being Thursday.

Not a problem, he replied.

Then they'd take the body away.

Our conversation was not easy. He spoke softly, and his Chinese-inflected German seemed to have been learned in school. My American-inflected German had been picked up—as far as that could be said of it—from friends and books. I strained to think of the right word for cremation.

They'd take him to the graveyard? he asked.

Yes, I suppose so. You're doing a burial? Or a—

Burial. Would you come along to the graveyard with me?

No. We would just do the ceremony, and that would be it.

He thought about this, then said, And the ceremony? I'm Chinese, you know, and—

Why don't we meet in person, Mr. Xiao?

Xiao.

Yes. I'll bring the text, and we can go through it line by line. I'll explain everything as well as I can. Would that be OK?

We agreed on a café and a time, and when we met, we ordered waters. I desperately wanted a beer, but didn't know how he'd feel about a potential funeral officiant who drank beer midday. I laid his copy of the funeral text on the table, mine next to it, and came around and sat almost beside him. His hair fell across his forehead to thick glasses. I hadn't yet been able to see his eyes or to make eye contact.

I knew, roughly, the Chinese names for the main deities involved, and he recognized them when I said them. As we talked, he seemed to relax. It became clear that whoever was in the majority, whoever owned whom, a common tradition of Buddhist funeral liturgy extended across the borders of China and Tibet. I showed him where in the ceremony I would ring bells, where I'd be reciting mantras, and I pantomimed the moving of beads. Here, I'd burn the picture—did he have a picture of the father? He did not. Calligraphy of the name and dates would serve. Did he want to write it, or should I? He would do it. And so on.

Monday morning Mr. Xiao called again, bothered by the part about the graveyard. He didn't want to go alone. Couldn't I come with him? Or one of us. I explained that despite our best efforts at gathering people, we were only going to be three. That was OK, he said, fine, but he was feeling very uneasy about riding out to the Westfriedhof alone, with the drivers and the corpse. I said I'd come. What about the others? he wanted to know. I said I'd call them.

When Mr. Xiao called back some hours later, he was pleased to learn that all three of us could accompany him and the body to the graveyard.

But then, he asked, couldn't we just do the whole ceremony out there?

Where?

At the cemetery. They have a building for it. Everything's there. We could just do the whole thing out there.

I imagined he'd been negotiating with the drivers and they had a per mile, per-stair price, and he'd wanted to keep all that to a minimum. This was understandable, but I made a mental note that Mr. Xiao and the Director should talk about the donation he'd make to our centre. With every change, and every phone call, that figure was rising in my mind. Saying goodbye to the rest of the day, I set about gathering the necessary materials, because although they had everything out there, they certainly had nothing of a Buddhist shrine.

For one thing, we needed a statue of Avalokiteshvara, the bodhisattva of compassion. This had been the name that calmed Mr. Xiao when he read it in the liturgy. We didn't have one in the centre. I thought it would need to be good-sized, something that took up some room. At the local Asia store I found one. The Avalokiteshvaras stood on the top shelf by the register, above the calendars, lacquerware, and ornamental swords. Harried-looking Chinese men lurking in the back of the store no doubt ran the place, but they put their attractive twentysomething daughters up front, on the register. When I asked to see the statues, the daughter on shift looked at me as though I were crazy: no one ever asked to see those. But she dutifully climbed up in her tight jeans and handed one down, and then another, and I set them on the rubber conveyor belt that moved groceries along to the register.

Which one?

What do you think?

That one. Definitely.

Why?

I don't know. It's just so much more… she opened her palms in front of her…you know?

I need it for a funeral.

Oh yeah, then definitely. That one.

She said Avalokiteshvara's name in Chinese, then added a few other things, possibly lines of praise from a chant she knew, as she made a few useless passes at dusting it off.

She rang the statue up, together with three magnums of sake and two bottles of hot sauce. Most of the sake was for an unrelated celebration at the centre, but she didn't know that. She kept looking from sake bottles to the statue to me and back to the bottles, but she said nothing. With shoppers in line making a kind of audience, we rolled up the bottles in Chinese newsprint, and wrapped the statue in bubble wrap. She helped me stow it all in the cloth bags I'd brought, for the hot, slow, careful walk home.

There, I gave the statue a lukewarm shower, praying none of the color would wash off. He/she—Avalokiteshvara's gender is intentionally vague—had a pretty, round face, and elegant hands and fingers, but the lotus seat looked gaudy to me. It was a hot pink, with extensive bright gilding. It would have to do. It was better than the statue we didn't have.

Tuesday the Director swung by to get me in his work van. He'd packed his tools and construction materials securely to the sides, to make room for the funeral kit. We both wore dark suits and ties; my ceremonial outer robe sat in its silk envelope atop the shrine materials for the ride.

Neither the Director nor I had ever been to this cemetery, nor, it turned out, had our third congregant, a handsome woman named Ellen. A longtime practitioner, she'd taken time off from her job to come watch and to help give voice to the chanting. We

parked as directed by signage and walked—miles, it seemed—
to the smallish funeral hall. The approach from the main gate
was another several hundred meters long, immensely wide, and
bordered with trees. It felt like walking into Versailles, and we
kept to the shade. We could see Mr. Xiao in front of the building,
pacing back and forth, smoking. He wore a dark-blue running
suit, and had on white sport shoes. As we got closer, he put out
his cigarette, and walked a couple of steps toward us, stopped,
and nodded. We nodded back. Behind him, a short, plump man
wrestled things from a hatchback car; he'd figured out how to
drive to the door, so I presumed he worked for the cemetery. Also
in attendance was the woman from the city's Mortuary Office.
She explained that she'd never seen a Buddhist funeral before,
and informed us we had about forty-five minutes. That much
time was reserved, but if we ran over, it wouldn't be a problem. I
told her we might. Not a problem, she repeated. Not a problem

Inside, the coffin was just immense—about the size and
shape of an office desk, constructed from a glowing brown nut
wood—and raised to about chest height. Walls of flowers flanked
it, left and right. Long, thick candles—real columns of white
wax—on wrought iron stands stood behind and all around.

We found a suitable table and set it between the folding
chairs—they'd put out about 100—and the massive coffin up
front. Ellen, the Director, and I rapidly assembled a shrine,
and found a side table to go by my seat, one that would hold
a gong, matches, and a wide bowl of powdered ash. This all
faced the audience, which, it became clear, was going to be Mr.
Xiao, Ellen, the Director, and the city mortuary woman. As we

worked, music began to seep into the room. The plump man with the hatchback had set up a keyboard, and was improvising dirges to go with our activity. We finished arranging things, and the statue didn't seem as big as I'd hoped. The woman from the city looked at her watch.

I had explained to Mr. Xiao at our meeting how I would burn the calligraphy of his father-in-law's name during the mantra recitation, and I'd shown him with my hands an appropriate size for the calligraphy paper. Mr. Xiao had gone several sizes bigger. Gauging that it might be possible to keep most of the burning, crumpling paper over the bowl of ash, I felt very glad that I'd opted to wear a suit instead of robes, with their sail-like, flammable sleeves. We had about twenty minutes left. We'll make it, I thought, since it was up to me to determine the length of our meditation, and because there was only going to be one person making a speech for the departed.

We took seats scattered around the room. From the back corner, the organist continued to play. Facing everyone, I nodded to the organist. This had no effect. He played along as though he hadn't seen me. I waited a few bars and tried again: raised my eyebrows and directed a theatrical, almost slow-motion nod his way. Nothing. I cleared my throat, gently. In my memory, he is rocking back and forth in a quiet ecstasy, working the pedals with his feet and massaging the keyboard with both arms. But this is probably an exaggeration. The options of drawing a finger across my throat, or forming and raising a T-sign with my hands didn't seem available. Ellen finally turned in her chair and began to rise, and this got his attention.

We commenced. At the designated point in the ceremony, Mr. Xiao rose in his track suit and running shoes and approached the coffin. He read in Chinese from prepared remarks. Parts of it seemed to be very emotional. It ran quite long. Having shifted in my seat to pay attention to him, I slipped into a kind of accountant's mentality: thirty-six pillar candles, each at least a meter-and-a-half long—bought? Or rented from the cemetery? The flowers, several hundred euros per side, for sure. Had they flown Papa over in the coffin? What did a Shanghai-Frankfurt flight run, for a corpse? And the paperwork? That coffin!

Such were my meditations. At last Mr. Xiao concluded his eulogy, and we worked through the text until we got to the mantra and calligraphy burning, the crescendo. Through the open door at the back of the chapel workmen suddenly appeared—five or six of them, as if cued by Shakespearean stage direction: Enter grave diggers at rear of stage. They stood around with shovels, wearing dirty clothes, waiting. Ellen, the Director, and I chanted the mantra—I think Mr. Xiao too—and with the good acoustics in there, we filled the chapel with sound. The card burned fairly cleanly. We kept going until the last corner of it turned to gray ash, fuck the workmen. Then I rang us out with two extended roll-downs on the gong. We rose as the echoes faded, and the workmen approached immediately, pushing a caisson up the central aisle. We got the ad hoc shrine, covered with crystal and porcelain, out of their way.

They slid the coffin onto the cart and towed it back down the aisle. Mr. Xiao requested that we accompany it. Ellen and the mortuary lady declined, but the Director and I followed the procession down a ramp out into the cemetery grounds. We proceeded through avenues of graves and monuments, all shapes and sizes—nothing old; this was a post-war graveyard. Some graves were in process: open, with dirt freshly mounded on the sides. The day was hot, but the grounds had been planted in flowering shrubs and shade trees, so the walk, though long, was not unpleasant. For us, that is. The workmen dragged their load without enthusiasm. Mr. Xiao paced a few steps behind them, sunk in apparent contemplation. We all walked silently.

At last we arrived at the plot. The workers slowed the wagon and looked at us as if to say, See? You understand? The hole was enormous and squarish, an empty sunken cube, its bottom lined with a cement floor and walls. The workmen positioned the coffin as best they could, and with thick canvass straps they slowly lowered it. They were sweating profusely. We all baked in the sun, but the Director and I only had to stand, as men anywhere will stand watching other men work. When they'd lowered the coffin completely, Mr. Xiao insisted that it be moved: centered, and squared up with the walls. Grunting and pulling on straps, they finally accomplished this. There was room in there for three coffins, side by side. Mr. Xiao then offered some flowers into the grave and spoke again. Now the workers went around behind the mound of soil and brought back what turned out to be the top half of a cement box. This they also lowered with straps, using the same hand-over-hand motion. Mr. Xiao walked around and barked at them until it fit the way he wanted. When it was done, he came down off a pile of soil and walked over to us. We shook hands briefly and inclined our heads to one another. He would stay as they replaced the soil; we would not. On the way back, the Director and I read names cut into the headstones.

Did he make a donation?

Not yet.

Did you talk about it with him?

I mentioned it. But I didn't suggest an amount or anything. Did you?

No. Do you think we have to call him?

Let's wait a couple of days, see what he does.

Back at the chapel we packed up, and hauled our materials out the long drive and around to the parking.

Shall we...

Yeah, I saw a place over there. A Greek place, I think.

They'd closed the kitchen, but served us beer out on the terrace. Our coats and ties hung in the van.

Boy, it gets to you, doesn't it, to see it like that. It really gets to you.

What does? I asked.

You know. Death. All those people who have died.

Yeah. I guess that's why it's a classic meditation, to go sit in a graveyard or charnel ground.

We drank quietly, and ordered more beer.

Did you see that thing? he said. It was like he'd built a little house in there.

Yeah, it was amazing. I paused, then thanked him for his help. I thought it went OK, didn't you?

Yeah. Maybe we should do more of those. You know, let it be known we do funerals.

Right. Now that we've got the statue, we could go into business: Buddhist funerals. It could get really big.

Maybe word will get around in the Chinese community. Then it really would be the next big thing.

You think?

They brought the beer out where we sat, heads not quite shaded by an umbrella, feet on bright green Astroturf. Just beyond the hedge that enclosed the terrace, a streetcar rumbled by, very close. The sound sent me into a kind of aerial view, a drone view: middle of nowhere suburb, graveyard, big road, streetcar tracks parallel to it, restaurant terrace up next to the tracks. Two dots on the terrace.

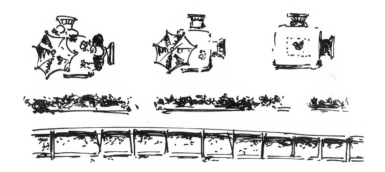

The Sword

*T*HE CEREMONY REQUIRED A SWORD, AND WE HAD NO
SWORD. We had a day, though. We thought we might find
a sword in the next town. The antique shops there sell decorative
weaponry, left over from the wars. It's not easy to meet up in a rural
meditation center, with everyone moving around purposefully, often
unpredictably, but the attendants and I see one another, and firm up
this plan. All we need is a car and a driver, and as we stand there,
along comes Alain—Parisian, patrician, handsome, moneyed, with
a big car and time to take us. Pleased to be asked, in fact.

He drives the two-lane road along the river. Trees and shrubs
line it so thickly it's like driving through a green-gold tunnel
sometimes, with glimpses of the river off to the left, and sudden
views of the pale, sloping fields to the right, red cows grazing on
them. We reach town midday. It had not occurred to us that on
this account the shops would be closed, but they are, for at least
two hours. We repair to a pleasant brasserie up a steep, dead-

end street in the area of the antique shops. Relieved to be away from the long food lines at the centre, with wasps hovering near the food, we sit outdoors and order aperitifs. A painful moment. Alain and the attendants drink *pressions*—large draft beers— while I, who love beer more than any of them does, regard my mineral water.

Two days earlier, I'd met with the teacher in his retreat, to go over the ceremony. Among other things, he'd given me detailed instructions on what the shrine servers should wear: which colors, which days. He also, for the first time I could remember, laid out a specific diet for them, one that prohibited alcohol. I'd finished writing all the points in my notebook, and looked up to see if there were more.

Oh, he said, you too.

Excuse me?

I'd like you to follow this diet too.

Me? I paused. I guess this means no beer, then?

He raised his brows, brightened his face, and asked, Can you do that?

Another pause.

If you're asking me to, I can. He named a date about a week away and said that if I could refrain until then, it would be good.

Because of the tilt of the sidewalk, Alain and I sit downhill at table from the attendants. They are both about twenty-five years younger than we are; neither is very large. The taller of them wears short brown curls that cling to his head the way it's shown in statues of Roman warriors. The shorter one has a modern military feel— buzz cut hair and tight musculature; he favors T-shirts. Both are very strong, with open, uncomplicated faces and manners, possibly owing to their being Canadian. Neither speaks much, except to each other, and then almost in code—a word, a phrase, or just a look between them. They'd been on the road for months with the teacher, and they'd worked so closely together that though they are two distinct young men, they feel like a unit. Alain and I invite them to lunch, and they order second beers, then wolf down substantial meals—steak (the red cows), potatoes, vegetables, salad—while Alain and I pick at fish. The boys order desserts and coffee.

Alain keeps rising from the table to talk on his *portable*. His business, the exact nature of which has always eluded me, is international. He is frequently in, or on the way to, or on the phone to, Colombia, Brazil, Thailand, Indonesia, Hong Kong, Switzerland. Something with minerals. It's all hours of the day for him, all the time. The constant travel, the only partly trustworthy associates, the large amounts of money to be made or lost—these stress him, and manifest in a continual series of health issues: backaches, gastric illness, the occasional facial tic. His work causes these, but so do his relationships with women, because Alain adores women. He especially prefers women of mixed racial descent. I've thought that he favored any *but* white European or American women, though I've met some of these too at his place through the years. I've also wondered whether it is really the women he likes, or the lethal undertow of being in love, feeling jealous, or being shut out of love—these extreme and absorbing states. He's been able to analyze it this way himself, though usually only from troughs of despair.

One time on a trip out from Paris to the centre, Alain had told me for two hours the circumstances, coincidences, little victories, confusions, and missteps that had led to his current heartbreak. He'd poured it into my hungry ear. At a rest area, we'd walked past the picnic tables, into ankle-high grass, and peed toward the woods beyond. As we stood there side by side, he used his free hand to fish his *portable* from his jacket, and to show me how she looked, clicking through the first few pictures of her, then handing me the phone. There were eighteen shots in all. Between zipping up, and being careful where I placed my feet, I looked. She was as beautiful as described, with freckles where he said they'd be, but she was clearly too young for him. In fact, her mother's stark disapproval had finally quashed their connection. (Alain had also had a liaison with the mother some years earlier.) I'd handed him back the phone, and seen he was crying.

You think I should erase them?

This hadn't occurred to me, but there was no future in it, and I told him so. He'd erased the pictures, one by one, taking longer with some than others. Back in the car, I watched as he also erased from the sound system the songs that had coded and accompanied their affair. He might hear those songs on the radio or in shops, he'd told me, but after two glum months of listening to them, driving himself to depression and desperate phone calls, he was going to cut it.

Now he comes back to the table smoking a cigarette, and he and I pay the bill. We make our way down the rough-cobbled street to the bottom, go left for one block, then climb back up a parallel street where the antique stores are. In the window of the first one, below a dark-blue, frayed uniform on a stand, we see what looks to be a perfect sword, the blade maybe two or three feet long. It's reminiscent of a bayonet, but it's a real sword, a short saber with a guard over the grip. It lies there in the window, next to a leather scabbard. This feels too easy, but we all enter the cluttered store to inquire. The proprietor, a bent older man, seemingly displeased to have customers, explains to Alain that the scabbard is what makes this one valuable; it's a complete set, and the scabbard is in mint condition. While they talk, each of us in turn holds the sword in our right hand and waves it as much as the cramped, stale space of the store will allow. Tomorrow the teacher will have to hold it and dub several hundred students. The attendants are concerned that he should not be overtaxed by this one part of a long, complex ritual. Still, the sword should be impressive. With the slightest nod of their heads—not much more than a blink—they indicate that this sword would be OK. Alain and the proprietor make first moves in the discussion of price. The scabbard comes with it, absolutely— this is not a point to be discussed.

With the sword on hold for one hour, we continue the search, up one side of the street, back down the other, finding nothing else. There is one modern store, however—a different kind—and we look in there, though it is confusing. This place is much larger, and given over to a wide array of weaponry. The store is on two levels, side by side, joined by a short staircase. Rifles stand vertical on braces along several walls. In the middle of the floor are racks of jackets and waders, as well as boxes holding rubber boots and other outdoor clothing. A long glass counter divides the customers' area from the owners'; in it are hunting knives and other fixed blades, folding pocketknives, switchblades, and also handguns, both new and used. A ladder leans against the wall behind the counter, fixed to it with wheels in a grooved track. This slides left and right, we soon see, allowing the owner to climb up and reach the proper box of ammunition from the hundreds of them stacked there.

The owner and his wife greet us. He's a handsome, relaxed man, with a ready smile, wearing pressed pants, a pressed shirt, and despite the day's warmth, a light cardigan sweater, partly buttoned in front. He shows us the few swords he has. These are mostly ornamental blades: some in the Japanese samurai style, presented horizontally on lacquer stands. He also brings out a few Middle Eastern scimitars, one of which is curved both left and right alternately, giving the effect of flame, flickering. I ask about this one, because in the traditional iconography there are images of flaming swords. The owner names a reasonable price, and I mentally mark it as a second possibility. None of the others in our party will give it a look.

Outside again, we decide on the first sword, and Alain goes to the antique shop to bargain. Too much interest will doubtlessly raise the price, I think, so I wait outside with the attendants, who are growing restless. It's been a couple of hours since we left, and we didn't really tell anyone where we'd be. Eventually, though, we enter the old man's store as he and Alain are concluding the deal; it feels as if a storm has just passed. Alain points out, mostly to us, that the metal on the sword is dull and has some rust flecks. These can be polished away, he says, with an interrogatory glance at the proprietor, down at the weapons store, the one we just left. The old man nods. There's an electric lathe there, he tells us, and the owner will polish it up for a nominal fee.

So we head back to the switchblades and handguns, and I thank Alain for fronting the money. The program will reimburse him, I say (actually considering this matter only for the first time). Or the centre will. Or maybe the money will come from the teacher's private funds. All this he waves off. It's a gift, OK? A donation.

In the few minutes we've been gone, the feeling in the weapons store has changed. There are many more customers now, talking with raised voices. Alain makes his way to the owner, who holds a place by the register. His wife, petite but shapely, teeters around in heels, filling orders. Her tight jeans, her white shirt open a couple of buttons, and her climbing up and down the ladder raise the temperature. She's the only woman in the store. More men push in. They're large, mostly unshaven, and they smell of wine. Something else too. Maybe blood. They definitely have manure and some mud on their boots. It turns out that this is the afternoon before hunting season opens, and they are here for supplies.

For air and a bit of room, I go up the couple of stairs to where the bows and arrows are. Recurve bows and crossbows are on display, all layered, polished wood and taut line, all mounted with telescopic sights. Also standing there are instruments so complex they do not look like bows at all but rather—with their wheels and shafts and pulleys strung on multiple lines—like miniature engines of war from the fantasies of Leonardo de Vinci. Arrow tips of every size and design, sharp and clearly lethal, are arrayed like ocean shells against black velvet in another glass case. Suddenly light-headed—dehydrated, no doubt, from the lack of beer—I sit down quickly on the stairs between the store's two levels. Perhaps still light-headed after a few minutes, it seems to me, and not for the first time, that the path goes strange places. It would have been inconceivable to the nineteen-year-old college dropout I was when I began, that I'd be here now. I never would have expected—when I knocked on the front door of the City Center building my first day—that thirty-five years later, with something like the same heart, I'd be slumped on a couple of linoleum stairs under florescent light, in a crowded gun shop, in small-town France, on a spiritual errand.

The sword polishing is not going very well. Five minutes up against the lathe have indeed turned a coin-size area of the sword shiny and silver again. This has the effect of making the rest of the blade look even duller. We agree with the owner for now to just do a strip of the sword along the blade, and only on one side. Fifteen to twenty minutes, he estimates, giving the job to a tall young man who's emerged from the back. The assistants chafe at the idea of more waiting, though they say nothing. For the first time a look of concern, or possibly irritation, crosses the owner's face. I hear myself saying I would like to buy the other sword, the one with the flame-like blade, and I do buy it.

On the way back we take the highway, instead of the smaller, prettier roads. The town we've left sits next to a river, as most ancient towns do, and our land at the centre also borders this river, maybe ten miles downstream. The highway, though, cuts across hills in a straight line. There is no sense from this road that the whole area—the small, interlocking valleys, the natural glades, the ancient waterworks—are part of one system, ultimately a big valley, drained by a meandering river. The French have also been putting in roundabouts with great industry wherever country roads meet, and as we exit the highway and slalom through these, our perspective on the landscape spins, as if we were in a video game.

Finally, though, we wind down to the river and an old stone bridge. A car coming up the other way flashes us with his lights, and this concerns Alain. He's been driving fast, but not recklessly. He slows as the road flattens out before the bridge, and we soberly go across its one lane. At the other side, a police car sits angled so as to block all traffic off the bridge, and to slow cars going along the road parallel to the river. Beside the car stands a young policeman; the irritated skin on the back of his neck shows him to be literally hot under his collar. We stop and turn off the car. The river gurgles behind us. There is ambient insect noise, and trees stand quietly on either side of the road we want to take, with afternoon sun slanting off their leaves. It feels like—it is—the middle of nowhere, especially for a law-enforcement checkpoint. It's hard not to take this personally.

The assistants settle into wait-at-the-border mode. Traveling with the teacher, a golden-skinned Bhutanese, active in Asia, Europe, and the Americas, has given them practice at this. They seem to pull in the sphere of their presence and watch quietly. It's us, I think. It's us foreigners, gathering at the land centre. True, there are a very few houses dotting the road between here and our place. At one point these even become a village of ten or twelve dwellings around an old church. But the only thing really happening around here at present is that cars are accumulating in our parking lots, the day before the ceremony.

Parking lot is perhaps too grand a name for the sections of the fields and pastures bordering the road through our property. They've been mown and marked out with string, and are now filling with vehicles. Anyone traveling the one-lane road can, without slowing much, read the license plates, which are predominantly Dutch and German. The cars themselves are mostly German. The one we're sitting in is a white Mercedes. The policeman's car, a French model, is decidedly smaller than ours, and painted metallic light green. It seems to perch on the road like a bug on a branch. The whole valley was occupied during the war, and this was countered with an active, deadly resistance. Murder, revenge, torture, massacre of women and children—the abominations on all sides have not faded away, and because of grisly memorials, they will not. We in the car are French and Canadian. The centre is swelling with Germans.

The standoff in front of our eyes between Alain and the policeman, however, is not an international matter. Complying with the young officer's request, Alain reaches across to the glove compartment and fumbles there for too long, but produces papers. The officer studies these, and Alain, and asks for more papers, which at last Alain is able to give him. The policeman waves little bugs from his eyes as he reads. He bends down in his boxy, columnar hat, hands the papers back to Alain, and takes a good look in the car. We're tired, but reasonably tidy—shaven, neatly dressed. The car has French plates, French papers, a French driver who speaks proper French. With what seems like regret, the policeman straightens up and dismissively flicks us on our way. He's already looking across the bridge again.

At first we don't speak. It's quiet in the car and outside it. Following the curves of the river we gain speed, and can hear from the trunk the occasional sliding and clanking together of the swords.

Formal Practice

*T*HE WAY INTO THE MEDITATION ROOM WAS A NARROW HALL about thirty feet long, lined with tatami mats on each side. Sitters who'd arrived late, or those who had to leave early, practiced out here. There wasn't much room to walk between the mats, a yard, perhaps. When a period of meditation ended, those in the main room left their seats first, peeling off in a smooth pattern and walking silently out through this hall. They passed between the rows of practitioners here. These people had to stand next to their sitting cushions, back from the edge of the tatami, so as not to be continually brushed by the robes of the line walking past. I saw her first out here.

I was part of the exiting line, and because it had begun to slow and bunch up around the shoe rack, I was able to take more than a passing glance. She drew the eye in several ways. Her hair—golden, stiff, airy, fine—was swept back and out from her face, as though wind-blown. She wore a light-blue sweater and white shorts—that in itself was remarkable in a meditation center where, for sitting, most people wore ankle-length black robes. She also stood differently from those around her. To remain in this hall as everyone went past and noticed that you had been late had a kind of shameful feeling to it. It felt at least like an inspection. Most people here held the good posture of standing meditation, but with extra downcast eyes and a retracted aura. This woman had none of that. She stood proudly, the smooth planes of her face radiant, her eyes open, looking starkly ahead. Like a goddess, I thought. Like a statue. She could have been the figurehead on a British man-of-war.

She was in fact the newly arrived girlfriend of an artist who had been coming around the center for several weeks, and who had become something of a local darling. His artwork derived from early training as a luthier. He'd discovered a wood-rosin mixture that could take an exact impression—of a human hand, for instance—and hold it, without clinging to the hand. It could take an impression of a face without sticking even to the eyelids. These impressions would retain for a while heat transferred from the body to the rosin. Especially if they were backlit, these reverse masks, with their emanations, looked highly individual, characteristic, and weird. A roller run over the surface of the rosin would flatten it, and scramble the shading, readying it for the next impression.

Crawford was experimenting with scale and methods of presentation, but it was already clear from these early works that his art would be not only beautiful, but popular with all ages, and commercially successful. The heat of creativity was on him, and the magnetism of it. Not that he lacked any: he was tall and lanky, with a head of unruly brown hair. Pulled back into a pony tail, it revealed the angles of his face to be every bit as dramatic as those of his girlfriend. His face seldom rested in stillness, though, other than when he was meditating. He had a wide smile that lit him, and his brown eyes flashed with enthusiasm—for his work, for whatever he was saying, or more important, for whatever you were saying. This warm energy is what I saw whenever I looked up at him. I suppose he was handsome; he was obviously and easily attractive. I'd come to know him a little, as I too belonged to an artistic fringe around the meditation center.

Crawford and Jane, as this new woman was called, seemed an odd pair, though I knew my perception was influenced by wishful thinking. Crawford tended to move in an almost jerky way, except when he had something in his hands: then, as his long fingers turned whatever was there—a book, a bell, a sheet of paper I might have put there—he would click into a concentration so intense you could practically see it in the air. But he gangled over Jane when they were together. Her movements were smooth, unhurried, as if she simply enjoyed making them. I noticed this when he first introduced us.

We were waiting outside the dining room, for the open Thursday dinner. We'd come from afternoon meditation and the short session of bowing and chanting that followed. Dinner—at tables and chairs—would be silent for the first ten or so minutes, but until the dining room doors swung open, we could stand around chatting softly, like pre-dinner gatherings everywhere, except that half the people here were in black Japanese robes, and we lacked aperitifs.

Grady, this is my friend Jane, from back East. Jane, this is Grady. He's a printmaker.

How do you do?

She looked at my eyes, and slowly took my extended hand with hers, not smiling particularly. Her grip was warm, as mine, alas, was not; I'd sat beneath one of the slanted-open windows during meditation, and there'd been a draft. Her eyes were blue-green, and some freckles adorned the upper parts of her cheeks and her forehead. Her gaze dropped very slightly, and then her head.

Where have you come from, "back East"?

Rhode Island.

I suppose I heard her words, but what I remember is the effect the name had on her mouth, *Rhode* pushing her lips forward, and *land* causing her tongue to flick her upper front teeth.

Providence?

Another slight nod.

Someone tapped the wrought-iron plate suspended in the courtyard with a wooden hammer. The clank and the dissonant overtones meant dinner. Upstairs, a portable gong began circulating through the halls, making soft explosions of sound first from one side of the building, then the other, and mingling with the harsh clanking from the courtyard. The dining room opened, everyone entered, and I didn't see them again until after the meal. Upon leaving, Crawford waggled a long-fingered hand at me. Jane stood beside him and smiled a little, as if I were a thought that had momentarily amused her.

Developing his rosin trays meant Crawford came to the center less often. He had to travel to seek suppliers, he had to see gallerists and other distributors, someone wanted to make a film of the radiations as they appeared from a person's face in the rosin. He'd caught a wave, and he needed to ride it. If he did appear for the morning sitting, as he sometimes did, it looked as if he was capping a night of work. Sometimes both Crawford and Jane came to the afternoon sitting. Jane only came afternoons, maybe twice a week; she would usually stay for bowing and chanting, but not for dinner. If they were there at the same time, they would leave together. I presumed they lived together.

Crawford worked in a warehouse in a fairly rough section of town. You might go over there for lunch—the restaurants there were authentic, inexpensive, and good—but the territory was disputed by several gangs. Night visits were ill-advised, though not impossible. Crawford's was one of several workspaces in the building—or buildings: his warehouse connected internally with a neighboring warehouse. A number of the other craftsmen and artists working there had built living areas into their sections. I had not seen Crawford's domestic arrangements, though I'd been to his studio, and I'd visited, with a key, a communal toilet. This had meant walking through several halls, making left and right turns. On the way back, I'd gotten lost, distracted by the artists and the work I could glimpse in the other spaces.

One Saturday night I attended a party in the warehouse. Crawford had invited me, though the celebration largely took place in a neighboring atelier belonging to a furniture maker. It turned out I knew this man too; or rather I knew his face—dark-eyed, handsome, pensive. He also came to the center sometimes. The party was very populous and sprawling, but friendly enough. Dance music and several cases of beer had attracted people from all through the warren of studios. In what passed for the kitchen of the host's place sat a famous writer—a spiritual writer—talking quietly with the group who'd gathered around him at the table. This was tremendously exciting. It had long been rumored that Carlos Castaneda did not really exist, and that his books—fantastic, absorbing, mystical adventures—had been ghostwritten, pure fiction. He'd given almost no interviews, done no public readings, written no magazine pieces. Whoever had written them, the books were addictive: you devoured them, especially if you were in any way connected with a spiritual scene. The publisher was to be commended, because the author's extremely low profile had inflamed speculation and interest.

Yet here he sat, if the long-haired painter I'd been chatting with told me the truth. Not only was it Carlos Castaneda, she said, her round blue eyes slightly protruding, but what was in the books was real. Her girlfriend Erin had told her this, and Erin and Carlos were a couple. Right now, though, she said, stepping closer, letting her hip-length hair sway and brush against me, she was worried about that relationship. Erin had been dancing for a while with just one guy, and seemed in no mood to stop. Indeed, when we walked over to look, the woman she pointed out as Erin and the man Erin was dancing with seemed in a kind of two-person rapture. The man was the furniture maker, and I suddenly remembered his name was Clark. The Clark Ark, Crawford had said once as we passed this workspace.

Clark impressed me. I'd only seen him sitting still in meditation, and now here he was with good dance moves. He wasn't showing off for a crowd; Clark and Erin were locked into each other, and their gestures were only for each other. Sometimes they danced as partners, with hands touching. Clark would spin her and Erin would flow effortlessly from his hands out and then back into them, under his arms or hers, spinning and returning. Sometimes they danced farther apart, freestyle but linked. It was clear to all of us watching—Lynn, the long-haired painter, me, and a number of others—that we were seeing something special. A ritual—a courtship, perhaps—with all the stages accelerated by music. Clark and Erin looked flushed and beautiful. When the song stopped, they stepped toward each other, laughing and touching hands. When the next one started, their faces seem to explode in excitement, looking at each other, and off they went.

I walked back to the kitchen to get a beer, and for my new friend Lynn, a white wine. Castaneda sat there, sort of holding court, though sadly, at the kitchen table. I listened for a few minutes. Maybe it was all true, what he'd written. He spoke in wistful phrases, sometimes pausing, looking off, shaking his head. He seemed like others I'd known who'd been taken apart—by psychedelic drugs, or living alone in nature, or whatever—and been put back together, but not all the way back together. I took the drinks back toward the dancing and thought, *You may be a man of knowledge by now, you may even be a shaman, you may be the best storyteller since Charles Dickens, but tonight you have little chance.* I handed Lynn her wine. Erin and Clark had gotten into the materials of his shop. She danced with a double-sided Japanese hand saw in one hand, and a bowl of wood stain in the other. Clark held an acetylene torch, and swung the cable the way a cowboy swings a lasso. He wore a welding helmet, with the visor up. Apart from these two, the dance floor had completely cleared. The slow, syncopated bass and choppy rhythm guitar of a reggae tune gave them the beat now, as they neared and pretended to threaten each other with the tools, or as they backed off and pretended to cower.

Lynn hooked her free arm in mine and turned me away from the dancing to ask who Crawford was. The rosin-tray maker? Apparently, the party was a goodbye/good luck for him, as he'd been invited to a residency in North Carolina. He'd be there for six to eight weeks at least, Lynn told me, adding that she had this from Erin. I hadn't known it, and I hadn't seen Crawford, I realized, since greeting him upon arrival. Then he'd stood by the door with a group of people I hadn't known, acting not only as host, but probably also as a kind of door-watch. Jane had not been with him. I hadn't seen her all evening. There must have been a hundred people by now, maybe more. It was difficult to judge in such a large space, not all of it lit up.

Someone began to project films on one of the large, structural warehouse walls. These were confusing, with two or three streams of crudely shot images running side by side, disjointed from one another. The film or films mixed ghastly sights—people cutting themselves, chewing razor blades, blood flowing—with images of pretty people kissing, disrobing, and making out, both hetero- and homosexually. It was hard to look, and hard to turn away.

I would like to meet Crawford, to congratulate him, Lynn said. And then I'd like to go. Do you think you could walk me to my car?

I'd be delighted, I replied, noticing that she had a touch of a Southern accent.

Nothing else had stopped just because the films had started. Dance music still boomed; people talked or shouted now, and laughed and drank in groups under bare lightbulbs along sheet-rocked corridors leading to the bathrooms. Someone was smoking weed.

We finally located Crawford in a low room, set up as the projection space for the films. Although his head nearly touched the ceiling, he had his big sunny smile on, and waved us in. The first thing I saw as we entered was that Jane was with him, looking beautiful, but oddly formal in a black cocktail dress and a string of pearls. I introduced Lynn, though it was awkward since I hadn't yet learned her last name. She enthused to Crawford about the rosin boxes in what was now clearly a drawl. Crawford in turn asked politely about her painting. While they spoke, I turned to Jane and told her how great she looked. A faint ray of pleasure seemed to lighten her face, and she performed her usual slight nod. Possibly because she seemed so dressed up, her movement came across as a kind of curtsy. Before I quite knew what I was doing, I had taken her hand in both of mine, bent, and kissed it. She had not resisted. As I rose from this little theater and looked up, she held my gaze for a second, tilted her head, frowned, smiled, and continued to regard me.

There was no scheduled meditation on Sunday morning. This had been so for about two months, and we who lived in the center were not quite used to it.

When he said a day off, our director reported at a house meeting, I never thought it meant a day off from *that*.

Glances bounced around the room; eyebrows went up.

But yeah. No sitting on Sunday morning. No wake-up bell. No nothing. Breakfast eight to nine. Bag lunch materials will be set out.

So when I came awake without the alarm clock this Sunday, I could lie there for a few minutes, as I usually could not. I had the luxury of watching impressions from the night before parade through my mind. The grisly film images on the wall; Castaneda with a series of beer bottles before him on the table; the spectacular tool-dance; the feeling of Lynn's long hair, and her cashmere dress and the skin of her back beneath it as we hugged goodnight at her car—when these and other thoughts had come and gone, the one that remained, the one that returned throughout the morning was Jane's green-eyed gaze.

Jane continued to come to the afternoon sittings, and after one of these she accosted me. Where had I been yesterday morning? She had had a late night and had come over for the early period. What kind of sitter was I, sleeping in, not showing up? Pleased that she'd noticed, I explained that on Tuesdays, Thursdays, and Saturdays I did not in fact come to the meditation hall. I drove a truck instead, a rather large one, down to the produce terminal, where I did bulk shopping for fruits and vegetables for the center's several residential locations and businesses.

Where is it, this produce terminal? she asked, after considering this.

It's south of here. I generally go on the freeway for about ten minutes, then I get off and go east. It's down in an area where there isn't too much else, I don't think—warehouses, train tracks, empty lots.

Are you close to the water there? Any of the piers?

Not too far. I mean, it's a drive, but not a long one. It depends on which number pier.

She named one, and explained that for a couple of weeks,

since Crawford had gone east, she'd been waitressing in an all-hours diner on the water.

Maybe you should come by there one morning after shopping. The breakfasts are OK.

The truck was much in demand, especially mornings; it usually wasn't possible to keep it past eight. But the center was about to hold one of its daylong retreats, and no one had signed up for the truck until 10:00 a.m. on the coming Saturday. So that morning I went to see Jane.

Laden with crates of oranges and lettuce, boxes overflowing with sloppy cabbage leaves and broccoli, flats of apples, burlap sacks of onions, thick, sewn-up, sixty-pound paper bags of potatoes, and some loose winter squash, I drove along deserted streets in the industrial district toward the water. Finally, rolling as slowly as possible over a set of train tracks, I entered a fenced and gated loading area. There I saw Dominic's on the Dock, the only lit-up place in miles. If locating the diner had been a chore, parking was blessedly easy. Dominic's sat on the extreme edge of a functioning pier. Things had been laid out with trucks and trailers in mind, so there was plenty of room. The café itself had an L-shape: half of it was on land and half jutted out over the water, supported by pilings and surrounded by a plank walkway. Stairs descended from this to a lower walkway at water level, along which were docked several boats.

I took a seat on a swiveling stool at the counter and watched as Jane and another waitress patrolled the rooms with coffee pots. They wore uniforms: pink seersucker dresses trimmed in white at the collars and at the short sleeves. Jane had cinched a white half-apron at her waist and somehow gathered and smoothed the material of her dress so that it fit her well. In her hair she wore what would have been a tiara if it had been made of jewels. This appeared to be only a piece of the same cloth as her dress, stiffened and affixed to a barrette—a little waitress crown. He cheeks were slightly ruddy from working, and she wore a smile.

Did you come in your big truck?

She poured coffee into the mug at my place. Without waiting for a reply, she emptied all but the dregs, placed the pot on top of the coffeemaker, hoisted a full pot from the middle of the machine, and returned. I had never seen her move so much or so rapidly. The gestures that had struck me as hypnotic when slow had, with the demands of the job, melted into a full-bodied grace. She topped off my mug from the fresh pot, extracted an order pad from an apron pocket, and looked me in the eye.

Take your order, mister?

What's good?

Try the Spanish omelet.

OK, then. With hash browns and sausage, I replied. No meat was ever served at the center. If you wanted any, you got it when you were out.

White, wheat, or sourdough?

I watched her take the order to the kitchen, and though I busied myself trying to straighten out order slips I had collected, and to match them against the receipts from the market, what I really did was continue to watch her. She had good field awareness as she circulated. She chatted in an easy manner with the men she waited on, and at this hour, the clientele spread around the place was exclusively male. I heard plenty of laughter and a steady rise and fall in volume as Jane and the other waitress engaged their customers, but nothing crude. If these men were like those at the market, they could be extremely—often hilariously—off-color in an all-male setting, but courteous with women on the scene.

One morning, very early, I had taken the head cook from the center's restaurant to the market. She'd wanted to see for herself where the fruits and vegetables came from, and the salesmen had practically fallen over themselves demonstrating chivalry. This included a good deal of sidelong mockery.

You know what? George began. I'll save you the sweetest citrus—grapefruit, lemon, orange—try a piece of this. No one else will have this fruit yet. It's good, no? And if you call me, I'll give you the best price. Now try this. You ever taste fruit like that? This guy—pointing a thumb in my direction—he's nice enough, except I don't know what happened to his hair. But let's imagine that he had some. He'd probably be OK.

While he spoke, George had opened a long-bladed folding knife from his coat pocket, sliced and peeled an avocado, and extended sections of it to her on the open blade. He'd also winked.

Delicious, right? I got boxes and boxes of these. Isn't that a good-looking avocado? Now see, this young man, I have to give him market price. Word might get around if I didn't. But ma'am, if you call me—wait, here's my card—you call me direct. Ask for George. Your boy here can still come by, pick your things up. But if you want a deal, you call me.

This had all taken place at the first house in the market, within about three minutes of our getting out of the truck. We had eight or nine more houses to visit. The talk had gone on like that the whole time, framed by handshakes, lifting of hats, sweeping of arms, and standing bows.

Jane set down the plate of food and poured more coffee.

There you go, she said, with a smile and one of her maddening tick-too-long looks. No one else would have noticed it, probably. Maybe she gave looks like that to everyone. Maybe I only hoped it. The sun was just rising over the hills on the east side of the water. It was beginning to glint off the little waves on the bay. A breeze blew through the window—fresh air off the water with a hint of gasoline. The day was just cracking open, though I'd been up working for hours. When she returned to clear my plate, Jane stood a minute and toyed with the strings of her apron.

I get a break in about fifteen minutes, if you've got time.

I have to get the truck back. I'm sorry.

She stood a minute, pulling on the ties, not saying anything.

Would you like to have dinner this week? I blurted. Maybe after sitting one evening, we could go out?

She raised her gaze, raised her eyebrows, took the plate, and nodded yes.

We neglected, in our shock at abruptly making a date, to specify the day. Calling would be difficult. Crawford had gotten his mail through his gallery; I don't know where he'd made phone calls, if he did, because there was no line at his studio. My situation wasn't much better: there was one phone on which center residents could take calls. This sat, with a lock on its dial, by the front office. Whoever was secretary that day answered it during office hours, sitting right there by it, and could not help but hear whatever you said. Whoever picked up this phone during non-office hours was a matter of chance. There were also two pay phones for the building's fifty residents.

Jane did not appear at meditation on Monday or Tuesday

afternoon, but she showed up on Wednesday. When people had mostly gotten their shoes and cleared away after the bowing and chanting, I found her sitting on a bench in the alcove, tying up elaborate boots. She straightened up from these, ran her fingers through her hair, and let her elbows float well out. Her gesture seemed to start out as a spinal stretch and develop into a yawn, one she only partly bothered to suppress. The effect was leonine. She saw me approaching, blinked a couple of times, and said, Tomorrow. Realizing that this would be the extent of her conversation, I nodded and shuffled off in my sandals to dinner.

Thursday after practice, I changed out of robes in my room, while Jane waited downstairs in the front hall and dealt with her boots again. She was coming out of the ladies' room when I got back. I held the front door of the center open for her, and she led the way to her car, which turned out to be a canary-yellow VW bug, convertible. We fumbled a bit at her car door; she unlocked it, and then I held it for her as she got in.

I'm not used to anyone holding doors open for me.

Can't help it—sorry. I was raised that way.

She'd still only been in the city a few months, and asked if we could go up to the highest peak for a look at the view before dinner.

We'd better go right away, then, I replied, because the fog starts to roll in soon.

Do we have time to get a bottle of wine on the way?

A little while later we sat parked with a few other cars up there, looking east, at city streets spreading down to the bay, at the blue bay itself, then at the freeways, campuses, cities, houses, and hills on the east side of the water. The light was clear enough this dusk to see, though faintly, a mountain behind the eastern hills. We got out of the car, and I pointed out to her where she lived, and where I did. A stiff wind blew, making it chilly, and blowing her hair around. I used the corkscrew on my pocketknife to get the wine open, and failing glasses, we drank directly from the bottle. After a few swigs, we walked to the other side of the parking area and looked west. Here we saw the dark treetops of the park—a manmade forest bordered by grids of parallel streets running out to the ocean. Cottony fog was coming in; you could see a massive wall of it approaching. *The march of the cloud gods,* I thought, as the wine began to land. Back in the car, we drank some more.

She suggested we eat at a Panamanian place she had seen on her way to work. As we descended the hairpin turns of the road, I noticed how well Jane drove. She seemed almost united with the car, and she clearly enjoyed accelerating through the curves.

You drove this across the country?

Yes, but it took a while. I stopped to see people. The radio gave out around Kansas.

What radio?

There was only a wound with a few straggly wires where it should have been.

Oh. That happened out here. In our charming neighborhood.

Her saying 'our' prompted me to ask about Crawford, since she and I lived in different dangerous neighborhoods.

He sounds OK. He's going to stay another couple of months.

Really? I said, tipping up the bottle of wine. I didn't want to think about Crawford. She nudged me with an open hand, and I passed her the bottle. After taking a sip, she put it between her legs, bunching the cloth of her denim skirt. We'd mostly come down from the steepest part of the hill, but she still had to shift. I wondered, but didn't dare look, how the bottle would do as she depressed the clutch and worked the gas.

Can you sing? she asked.

What?

Can you sing? I was thinking that since I don't have a radio anymore, you could provide some music.

A little, I guess. Do you care what?

Maybe because we were going to a Panamanian place, Ry Cooder's album *Chicken Skin Music* came to mind.

She shook her head briefly, so I began to croon—I think that's the only word for it—the sad song titled "Yellow Roses" from that album. In my mind I heard the slow pedal steel guitar, and I crooned along with that. About the third or fourth line in, I glanced over at Jane. She turned her head slightly, eyes still on the road, then swiveled completely and spat a mouthful of wine on me. My imaginary backup band stopped playing.

Oh, my god! she said, as her eyes got very wide and she began to laugh. I'm so sorry. I didn't mean to do that.

Hmm? was all I could manage. She swiftly pulled the car to the curb, extracted a handkerchief from her bag, and began to wipe the wine from my face and neck.

Listen, if you don't like what I'm singing, all you have to do—

No, no! I liked it! It was pretty. And sweet. She patted my shirt to blot the stray flecks. It's only that it was *too* pretty. I wanted to add another element.

So I'll warn you when I get to the chorus, OK? Because that's *very* pretty. Just in case you want to add more elements...

Her eyes looked beautiful and bright-green as they surveyed the wine-sprayed area. She put a hand behind my neck and leaned up and kissed me fully on the mouth. It was brief; it had a definite end, but it was a real kiss. Her breath was sweet with wine.

I'm sorry.

At this moment, perhaps in response to it, my nose began to leak. I sprang a prodigious nosebleed. Jane unballed the handkerchief from her hand and wedged it between my lip and nostril commanding me to lean back. I'd had episodes—periods, really—when this had happened to me, so I knew what to do. I tilted my head toward outside the car and told her I had to lie down. As luck had it, we were alongside a park, one with a slope down to the sidewalk. Checking the ground carefully, I positioned myself across the grass so that my head was slightly downhill. Jane rummaged in the back seat of her car and emerged with a roll of paper towels, one of which she exchanged for the handkerchief. She'd also brought the wine, which she now sipped.

Do you want any?

Not at the moment, thank you. This'll take about five minutes.

She sat beside me and drank some more. Your blood is a pretty color, you know.

Yes, when it first comes out. It never looks as good, though, when it's dried.

This is where we were when the cloud gods caught us. They'd hit the peak and other hills of the city, and rolled over them, somersaulting down inland, like soldiers coming over the battlements of a besieged fort. In the park lights I could see the fog moving eastward, above and around Jane's hair, as I lay there, bleeding and looking up at her.

Dinner was kind of a blur. From the cocktail list we'd each ordered one of the featured drinks. I had a rum-and-Coke made with their house overproof rum. It didn't taste that strong, and I was distracted in any case by trying to make conversation with Jane. But when she left to go to the ladies' room, I felt, sitting alone, as if I'd been fixed to my chair with circus tent pegs—tent pegs hit with a broad-head wooden mallet. Of course, I'd also tasted her drink—a milky-sweet concoction based on a kind of cane alcohol. We had an inconclusive discussion about rum and cane alcohol. I do recall that the meal was plentiful—big, warm plates on which the meat was flanked by rice and beans. It was salty, I remember, which meant beer. Or, in my case, I'm afraid, several beers.

The studio warehouse sat between the restaurant and the center. It seemed only natural that we should stop there, so she could show me some of her artwork. She had not set up a proper workspace, she said, because handmade paper required a lot of room. She did have some examples she'd brought from back East, and some early attempts at marbling. It felt equally natural, with our guards down as far as they were, that I should take her hand as we walked the half block from her car to the door. Inside, we continued holding hands as she led me through the series of turns to Crawford's studio. She put her jacket over a chair, and her bag beside it, then hoisted from under the central work table a very large portfolio, tied closed with ribbons. This she placed on the table, opening it like an enormous book. I stood next to her as she turned the big sheets of paper and looked at her work. I admired her watermark, which she said she'd developed from the medieval sign for chemical alum. It didn't mean anything; she just liked the shapes.

At one point she leaned forward to flick away a speck of something from the top of a sheet, and I put my hand on her lower back. When she straightened up I left my hand there, then I gently slid it further around her. So we stood for the next couple of sheets, until I finally turned my back on her paper, leaned against the table, and, with my hands on her hips, pulled her toward me. She came forward and we began kissing, tentatively. It is impossible to say whose lips opened first, whose tongue touched whose lips first, even though it seemed to take place in slow motion. When she opened her mouth completely and came forward, it felt as though everything opened. The room disappeared and her body was against mine. It is also impossible to say for how long we kissed, or who broke it off so we could look at each other. It is possible to say the look was brief before we resumed kissing. After a while I kissed down her throat, and up the side of her neck to behind her ear, where her hair began. It scratched and tickled my face. With fingers apart I traced down her back and held her at the waist, fingers pointing to one another across her low back, thumbs open in front, pointing toward her navel. I gripped her as though to lift her, as in ballet partnering, then relaxed my hold. I say this as though I was doing it, but it didn't feel that way: my hands were doing it; my lips were just doing it. Now I could feel a pulse begin in my whole body.

Come on, she said, breaking our embrace and leading me through the workroom to a short hall, off which were other curtained-off rooms, with a rough-hewn staircase at the end. This we mounted to a second-story bedroom. Trunks and boxes sat neatly along its walls. An armchair rested in the room, a lamp standing over it. The lamp's cable snaked over the plywood floor to an industrial socket. An imperfectly rectangular, body-length mirror leaned against a wall.

Wait up there. I'll be right back. She indicated that I should climb farther, up seven or eight feet on a ladder. I presumed that at the top was the bed, the sleeping platform. The bottom of this platform sheltered the reading area.

Is this where you and Crawford live?

She was looking in one of the boxes, rummaging with both her hands in it.

We're not really...together, she said as she continued fussing with her hands in one box, while beginning with her eyes to look at another. I waited, but she added nothing. The word *together* then, as she'd said it, remained in the air, draped in some kind of disdain. I went over to her and put my arms around her, which she ignored.

Go on. Climb up. I'll be right back.

Gathering from the several pairs of shoes at the foot of the ladder that I should remove mine, I did so, and also left my jacket over the chair before climbing up. I was unsure about the rest of my clothes. I didn't want to presume too much. On the other hand, it felt odd to lounge fully clothed on someone's private sleeping quarters. And why else was I up here? I decided on underwear, and folded up my pants and shirt, stacking them off to the side on a relatively uncluttered, smooth wooden plank that ran around the sides of the mattress. The bed platform had been set into the corner, and had no railing on the two open sides. The ladder just leaned up against it.

Immediately I felt drafts, and thought about getting under the cover. Without Jane here, that felt like an invasion. I put my feet under a blanket across the foot of the bed. I tried to feel casual, but I was not used to unstructured waiting time in bed. I hadn't had a girlfriend in a while, and in my own bed, back at the center, I was either sitting in meditation posture for a few minutes before sleep—one of the ancients had recommended this—or I was flat-out unconscious. I was rarely there for six hours at a stretch anyway, usually less. Finally, I pulled up the cover and just lay on Jane's bed, vaguely queasy, looking up at the corrugated metal roof.

When she walked back into the room she was naked. She walked with the same slow pride I'd seen in her posture that first time, in the long hall outside the meditation room. Though she wasn't tall, her legs looked long as she crossed the room, putting one foot in front of the other, and climbing the ladder. As she got near the top she looked up at me, who was transfixed by watching her. Her breath smelled fresh, and her skin was cool as we got under all the covers. She rubbed her feet against my legs. We took back up with making out, and soon we were both more than warm—warm enough in any case that I could pull the covers back and just look at her.

She turned her head to the side as I did, though her eyes slid back to watch me. In the warehouse full of artists' studios, I really wished I could paint, or sculpt. She was so beautiful it literally ached in the middle of my breast. I ran my hands very lightly over her skin and her contours. Fine blond hairs shone on her arms and legs, like down, or pollen. My palms and fingers lightly rubbing her breasts caused her to gasp, and turn her head back straight. She shivered or convulsed slightly and reached out for the cover as I stroked the smooth skin of her torso. I lay down again with her and began to kiss everywhere my hands had been. She caressed my head as I did. Then I pulled the cover up over us both, and went down on her. Her body contracted slightly into a C-shape, but there was nothing in her hands telling me to stop. I felt them open and close a couple of times, like butterfly wings, pressing back hard on my skull as her fingers closed. I regretted that I couldn't see her face, with mine buried down there. There was nothing of chivalry or politeness in what I was doing. I'd just been overrun by sexual greed. I understood why, in several languages, people said *eat* for this.

I put my hands under her and lifted her slightly to my mouth. From there, I let her guide me, and did what she told me to with my fingers. After some time of this, things got very jerky. Her breath and movements suspended, then continued again, very quickly. Then again, it was as if she held her breath, and stopped. I could feel her muscles contract. Finally, she released, with a loud, repeated Oh! Oh! Oh! I stayed where I was. For all that anyone could see it, I was smiling. Her fingers continued to press and relax on my head.

After resting like this a while, she reached farther down and cupped the back of my head in her hands, to pull me up. We looked at each other, and her eyes got wide again. She reached up behind her head for what looked like a T-shirt, and began to wipe the considerable dampness from my face. Her eyes snapped into focus, and her movements were deft, precise, and somewhat forceful.

I thought I was through.

What?

After looking my face over, she said, That's the second time tonight I've wiped blood off your face. Only this time it was mine.

Really? Are you sure? I could feel a touch of pride begin: this act, after all, was reputed to be part of the initiation into certain motorcycle gangs.

Well, there was no blood running out of your nose. And mine's a little darker, anyhow.

That's fine, I said. I lay on my back and she lay on her side next to me, an arm across my chest, with her face in the crook of my neck and shoulder. Soon, though, she began to rock gently against me, her arm and hand descending across my chest and stomach. Finally she took me in her hand and began to stroke and pump me.

I think I may have drunk too much tonight, I confessed. Too many different things, too much altogether.

Hmm.

She pulled the cover back and kissed my nipples. Then she kissed all over my abdomen, and then she took me in her mouth. I say *me* because by the time she got down there, that was me. All that there was, all that counted in that moment was there in her mouth. I responded to her attentions, and soon had to warn her I wouldn't be able to take much more. I wasn't sure she could hear me, so I ran my fingers through her hair, but she took my wrist, removed my hand, and pinned it on the mattress. She quickly finished me the same way I had her. She stayed there, keeping me until the numerous spasms and aftershocks had faded, and then she came back up to lie as she had been, by my side, with her arm across my chest. This time I managed to get an arm around her as well.

Thank you.

She didn't say anything.

Shall we pull the cover up? It's kind of drafty.

She pulled the cover up and I lay there in pleasant shock. A few hours ago, I hadn't so much as touched her hand, and now all this had happened. Here she lay, comfortably next to me, as if she and I were used to it. My thoughts tried to assemble themselves, but the alcohol, food, and sexual release gang-tackled me, and the next thing I heard was a raspy grunt, a horrible half-snore—mine.

What time is it?

Not moving anything but her arm, she reached behind my head, took her alarm clock, and put it down on my chest. It read 3:10. Meditation began at 5:00, and sitters needed to be in their places by 04:55. We were doing a Practice Period; attendance would be taken. At the very least *my* absence would be noted, since the produce shopping mornings already halved my time in the meditation hall.

I should probably go soon, I said. After a few seconds she sighed, and groaned, and yawned more or less all at once, but in a tone that definitely disapproved.

No, really, I have to be there this morning. I calculated that I could get from where I was to my seat in the hall if I walked, without rushing. But I'd have to start soon.

I'll drive you.

What? No. Stay where you are—it's nice here. And you look beautiful right where you are.

I'm not going to be able to sleep right away, anyway, so I might as well take you. Just wait here a minute.

She climbed down the ladder and disappeared from the room. I drifted off.

OK, let's go. She rattled the keys, holding them out with her arm extended, dangling them from the ring. She was still naked.

Jane, you're not dressed.

I know. I'm going like this.

Are you kidding?

No.

Please put something on.

She turned and walked out of the room. I fumbled around in the covers for my underwear. Jane walked back into the room, wearing her tie-up boots. They came up over her ankle, but again, this was all she was wearing.

Jane! I said this in two tones, making it a complaint.

What? You said put something else on. I did.

OK. Now please put something else on. We're going out. Please. Come on.

She turned on her bootheel and went out. I shakily descended the ladder. When she returned, she had added a leather jacket to her ensemble—keys, boots, and now a leather jacket. She hadn't bothered to zip it. Something in the way she stood there made it clear that this was it. She wasn't going to put on anything more and she didn't want to hear anything more about it. I finished dressing quickly, and then, indeed, we went out: down the stairs and eventually onto the street. In the studio, and the warehouse corridors, Jane walked at a stately pace, no hurry at all. She did not vary this on the street. I looked around but didn't see anyone else. When we got to the car I again held her door as she got in, thinking this time about the plastic material of the seat. She drove us in her authoritative way, leaning a little forward over the steering wheel, as if to see better.

In front of the center, she stopped in the middle of the street and put on the parking brake. She left the car running. Abandoning lookout duties, I opened her jacket and kissed her body some more. It was night, but the streetlights, high up, cast a pinkish-yellow hue. Finally I sat up in my seat, and we looked at each other, leaning against our respective doors. There was a smile in the air. Then she nodded once, definitively. I got out, looked up and down the street, then leaned back into the car to wish her luck with parking. She smiled some more and put the car in gear, pulling an unhesitating U-turn. When I couldn't see her car any longer, I got out my keys and went up the steps to the front door—to a shower, a fresh set of underwear, robes, a cup of coffee, and the formal practice of meditation.

Protection

T 06:30 WE WENT THROUGH THE LAST SERIES OF TURNS, rolled across a construction site with its piles of gravel and clodded earth, and pulled alongside the curb in front of darkened glass doors—the entrance to the VIP Lounge at Amsterdam's Schiphol Airport. The driver moved the car forward some and we got out to wait for the rest of our convoy. This morning, unusually, I'd ridden in the lead car. Mostly during this visit I'd ridden in the van with the monks, if there had been room, or in one of the cars straggling after. But there had been no rule, no fixed form; I might have ended up in any car, or I might have already been at the site, having gone on ahead independently.

The past ten days had seen us on a variety of events: large, public talks in churches; sightseeing visits to dikes or canals or museums; formal teas with the local Tibetan refugee community; days of interviews at the centre with media representatives; days of interviews at the centre with earnest spiritual seekers; a down day with no activities. The crescendo had taken place yesterday with the initiation—on the second day of a two-day ceremony—

of several hundred participants into a rare cycle of teachings, a body of liturgy and ritual held by very few masters, a transmission that His Holiness, until the very last minute, had been hesitant to give. I do not mean His Holiness the Dalai Lama. In Tibet before 1950, with its enormous distances between population centers, its terrain, weather, and the nonexistence of much mechanized transportation, a number of His Holinesses held sway, and they have continued to do so in diaspora. In the old country, residents of one area—necessarily followers of the school and style and leader of that area—might never have even heard of any other school or leader.

It's been a long campaign, eh?

Paul, driver of the lead car, looked sharp in his green blazer and dark-gray slacks, his tie and lapel pin—a city-duty uniform. The protectors, as we call them, take pride in their clothing. Wearing this outfit, they were formal but not showy; serious, but not threatening. When they stood together, you could see they were in uniform; individually, they just looked like respectfully well-dressed women and men. Under the knot of his gold tie, I noticed Paul had only had time to iron the part of his shirt that showed. Who could blame him—his days had been even longer than mine, and he lived well outside of town.

They'll be here in one minute, he said, punching some buttons on his phone. Even in the dim light, his eyes looked bloodshot. But then, I rarely saw his eyes; our protectors favor sunglasses whenever they can find an excuse to wear them. I got out the little bottle of drops I keep in my suit, put a couple of drops in each of my eyes, and offered Paul the bottle.

Later.

He pointed to a long, low car we'd rented to convey His Holiness. Paul positioned himself to get the car door, and signaled for the driver to ease forward. I backed up near the VIP Lounge door, and readied a white silk scarf I would again offer His Holiness. I wasn't sure if this was technically a white-scarf moment, but since the offering is a sign of respect, I'd decided to go with it. I had probably offered him this silk scarf a dozen times this visit. He'd accepted it each time, and given it back traditionally, draping it over my lowered head and neck. Each time, in an unobserved moment, I'd removed and stored it. As soon as possible, it had been refolded and rolled in one of the patterns I'd learned, so that it unfolded ornamentally like a cloud when I next offered it.

The folding and rolling had been imparted to me with great seriousness some years earlier by an older student who'd spent time among the high teachers. It had been a lesson. For a proper fold, two people were required; we'd rehearsed the offering, especially the gentle toss from one hand to the other, the holding, ducking the head, approaching smoothly. Again and again. The fact that no Tibetan teacher I'd ever seen offering a scarf to another Tibetan teacher had done this did not deter me. Their relaxed styles with one another were for insiders, I thought. What do we white kids know? Some of the teachers had seemed amused by my routine, but none had ever refused a scarf, nor corrected my form.

I was startled as I edged back toward the dark-glass doors by their suddenly sliding open. I must have tripped a motion detector.

Inside rose a short flight of stairs, with more glass doors at the top, transparent. Here stood another protector. She too wore a green blazer, over a dark-gray skirt. With black stockings and low heels she looked very natty indeed, especially for the hour of the morning. His Holiness emerged from the back passenger-side door, his translator/attendant climbing out the other side. HH (as I call him sometimes to others) stood a few seconds, adjusting his robes, not taking the arm one of the protectors offered him. He looked as he always did—rock-solid, despite his advanced years and the trials of decades in an Indian refugee camp. He'd built a monastery and a school there, largely on barren land, and the institutions now teemed with monks.

When teachers are credited with building monasteries or schools, it often means they sponsored the work, raised the money. This Holiness had done that, but he'd also built the place with his own physical labor, mixing cement, carrying hod, banging nails—whatever was needed. He'd worked alongside everyone else, or even occasionally alone. He was short, stout, and immensely strong. When I first saw him, he did not look like I imagined a Holiness should look. He wore squarish silver glasses under cropped gray hair. A smile so frequently creased his face that it was nearly impossible to see his eyes; they were horizontal lines, and they were anyway behind bifocals. I could easily picture him in short sleeves and a tie, in an air-conditioned office in, say, Tucson, Arizona, closing a deal for aluminum fixtures. He might volunteer at the school as wrestling coach.

On the other hand, when His Holiness sat in a chair to give a talk or have a conversation, or when he sat on a throne to conduct a ceremony, or even, somehow, when he walked, as he was now doing, leaning on the arm of his attendant, he conveyed a mountainous meditative stillness. This body-shaped field of stillness was now limping toward the sliding doors, so I stepped forward and offered the scarf. He stopped and, chuckling with his attendant, accepted it, returned it, and went on to position himself by the bannister before mounting the stairs. These he went up using the rail and his attendant, with a protector in front and one in back. The upper glass doors opened and the VIP Lounge people guided him to a seat.

The twelve-seater van arrived next, carrying nine monks. The senior one sat shotgun and greeted me with a big smile as he disembarked. He turned to watch his younger charges climb out of the van's sliding side door. We exchanged pleasantries: yes, yes, everything fine. Breakfast at the centre, yes, fine. Very good, no problem. With me he was always this way, unless he needed something for the monks, or unless, as on several outings, he was after something specific. For a few days he'd been looking for an eight-sided crystal. Had I seen one at any of the rock shops in town? He'd only found six-sided ones, and wanted an eight-sider. Also failing to find one, I suggested that perhaps eight-sided crystals did not exist here. Unamused and distinctly superior, he'd told me they definitely did, though they were rare.

With the other monks, he could be quite tough. He looked older than most of them—maybe thirty—and his arms were scarred with vaccinations. They were thick, as was his torso. He wore a thin mustache and a goatee, and when he spoke he commanded attention. The crystal business aside, we were on good terms.

The other monks were harder for me to distinguish. There

was one tall, willowy one, and a short, stocky one whose body had so much energy he seemed to bounce. He actually did bounce when he walked. But mostly I hadn't found time to get past the anonymity enforced on the monks by their identical robes and shaved heads. They were all along for different reasons, that much was clear; they had jobs, specialties. Half of them were musician-monks, responsible for the cymbals, horns, and drums of the long rituals. His Holiness was very particular about the music, insisting that it should be played absolutely right. He was intolerant of mistakes or lapses in attention. The blocky, bouncing monk specialized in horns, both the shorter ones—about the length of a soprano saxophone—and the really long ones, at least twice as long as he was tall. This was played with its bell resting several meters in front of him. His cheeks puffed out extremely as he played either horn, but I could literally feel the thunder of the long horns—a monstrous, mind-stopping blat—from my seat, which was very often in the front row because of my role.

Another corps of the monks had busied themselves with construction of the shrines, the hierarchical layers and risers of them, as well as with the ritual implements and dough sculptures that adorned them. The sculptures—of roasted flour, water, and butter—rose with astonishing precision and speed from the monks' uniformly graceful fingers. I'd had enough experience in trying to form these myself to know I was watching world-class dough sculptors. The shapely, svelte, quasi-anthropomorphic figures they effortlessly fashioned looked as though they'd been turned on a lathe. These were decoratively colored, dotted with butter, and extended with little sticks bearing ornamentation. My own attempts, even at much simpler representations, sometimes looked OK for a little while, but soon failed—sagging, melting, and deforming, so that by the time of their actual use in a ceremony, they resembled large squatting toads.

The shrine monks knew exactly where to place their sculptures on the shrine, when to bring them to HH, when and where to replace them. They moved unhurriedly back and forth, despite increasing liturgical complexity. Their gestures, as they raised, offered, or accepted things, seemed designed to soothe the eye of a viewer, almost to hypnotize a viewer into a state of composure. We in the front rows particularly needed to guard our alertness against too much composure, lest the relaxation lead us into a mortifying, head-rocking doze.

This morning, though, we were all sleepy and chilled standing about on the airport curb. After a last check in the van for possessions—especially passports—we clumped en masse up the stairs and into the VIP Lounge, where the airline staff lined people up and began to work on ticketing. HH was sitting in the middle of a small couch, his seat draped in brocade, with the spaces immediately left and right of him kept empty. His attendant stood by the couch. The monks began to take seats around the otherwise empty lounge, and I allowed myself a moment's relief; so far, it seemed to be going well. The head monk—mentally I called him Goatee, though his name meant Fearless Radiance— worked with one of the protectors so that the party's luggage was invisibly handled some other place, moving directly from curb to cargo bay. The monks traveled with few personal effects, but the ceremonial gear—robes, statues, paintings, instruments— made extensive freight. Each monk carried his own items in a cloth bag slung over a shoulder: usually some reading matter, a set of prayer beads, passport; some of them had wallets, some had little cameras. His Holiness had been given a stylish leather men's purse for such things, but mostly his attendant carried it, together with his own cloth one.

When everyone had settled, Paul and I approached the small, portable counter where uniformed stewards and stewardesses stood. We wanted to check about the flight, and about motorized transport for HH, should the gate be distant, but mostly we wanted to let them know that we were their reference points. They seemed to get this, and told us that as far as they knew, this morning's flight to Greece was on time.

A quarter hour later, though, a blond attendant, her hair severely pulled back into a bun, approached Paul and me as we stood in front of the complimentary food table, contemplating whether or not we could stomach warm cola. I'd had so far that morning a cup of hot water and a cup of instant coffee, hours earlier. I poured the cola into a glass and held it as we turned to the woman. It looked like the flight would be delayed, she told us. She wasn't sure why, but it appeared it would be at least an hour and a half. I drank warm cola from the glass. Possibly in response to my face, she said that the tea and coffee and breakfast items would arrive any minute, and that we should make ourselves comfortable. Paul's speaking with her in Dutch did not produce any further information. Paul and I approached HH's attendant and Goatee. Both were unfazed by the news, and HH only grunted gently and smiled when it was relayed to him. With their main monastery in rural India, travel delays were familiar. Beyond that, waiting—or its more classical name, patience—was a core virtue of monastic life.

Breakfast materials did in fact arrive, and after a cup of tea and a plate of food had been taken to HH, everyone else congregated at the table. The monks had no problem ordering themselves for service, but the protectors and I seem to confuse things. There was a great deal of bowing and gesturing to say, you-first-no-no-you-first-please before we worked it out.

Not long after, the airline rep with the severe hair, accompanied this time by a young steward wearing uniform pants, a white shirt, and company tie, came to see Paul and me. They weren't sure, they said, but it looked like the flight to Greece that morning might be cancelled. They hoped not, of course, and would confirm with us as soon as they could, but they wanted to at least give us this news now. When would the next flight be? Paul inquired. Hard to say. There might be one in the late afternoon, around 5:00. They wouldn't know until after 2:00 p.m. Of course, they hoped this morning's flight would still go, and they were dreadfully sorry for any inconvenience. We were welcome to stay in the VIP Lounge until things were sorted out. The young airline steward took a few steps toward their counter, leaned over to look at a monitor, then stepped back toward us to say that the flight had now indeed been canceled. They would be at the desk if they could be of further service.

I surveyed the room. It was close to 08:00. At this point we were HH, his attendant, Goatee, eight monks, Paul, some other protectors, and me. There were more protectors outside with the vehicles. It was hard to know how many, since part of their training was to be visible when needed and to fade into the background when that would better serve. The VIP Lounge itself was relatively barren: There were bathrooms, by them a rack for newspapers, not yet stocked with today's editions. There were a few TV screens around the room suspended from the ceiling, but these were blessedly blank at the moment. We had just indulged ourselves in the one entertainment the room offered—the buffet—and that surely wouldn't change for four or so hours. Besides, this being the Netherlands, it might not change much. Bread, rolls, butter, jam, cheese—these would surely stay. Probably the pastries would be replaced. There might be some sliced meats, some pickles; there might be colored and chocolate sprinkles. Paul went out to speak with the drivers, and I called back to the centre, to see if we could return there.

The centre director, when I finally reached her, told me in her breathiest voice that they were well along with takedown. The furniture we'd borrowed from an antique store had been wrapped, loaded into a van, and was on its way back, as promised. The monk's quarters, which had been simply but elegantly laid out dormitory style in the main shrine room, had been dismantled. Everything was currently out of the large room; it was being cleaned and would be reassembled as the main shrine room, certainly before this evening's open-house sitting.

I checked my watch again, wondering how they could have done so much. Then I realized a call must have gone out a day or so before, inviting anyone who could to assemble at the centre for a formal goodbye to HH and crew. Usually there would be a good crowd for the waving, and for the formal requests to return. There had probably then been a festive breakfast (I could imagine sparkling wine) to mark a big, hard, job well done. Given the remarkable hustle of our Dutch group, the breakfast cleanup had probably turned into a general work period, as people rolled up their sleeves and set about transforming the place from a monastic hotel to its usual role as a meditation-library–community center.

When I say she was breathy I don't mean to imply that our centre director was flighty or superficial; she was not. She had a habit of gasping, though, to signal she'd heard what you said—a sharp inhale, a light tone, and if you were together in the same room, a nod. All this to mean I *understand*. Sometimes she gasped at the end of things she herself had said, as people will sometimes nod at their own remarks, to encourage your agreement. She was not alone in her gasping. I'd heard it around in Amsterdam. Now, as I was giving her news that stressed us both, the gasping increased.

Cars are still here, Paul said, with a grin, as we met to exchange ideas. I guess we could take them all to the beach.

He was referring to an unplanned outing we'd had about three months earlier, having collected our teacher from this same airport after an overnight flight from San Francisco. Our teacher that morning had felt the need for fresh air, for stretching his legs, and possibly also for making trouble, in one of the few ways Tibetan incarnate lamas can get away with making it. This generally involves playing with the minds—especially the expectations—of whichever students are around. He'd been polite, hinting at first. We are not very far from the beach here, are we? How far is it to the beach, exactly? How long would it take to go there? No, from right here. Do you know the way? It's pretty much straight out this road, isn't it? Finally, we'd gotten his point.

At first, the luggage car, holding our teacher's traveling attendants, had stayed with us as we'd ignored the turns of the preplanned route to the residence, but at some point we lost them. The lead car had only noticed after several minutes that they were leading no one. With the crude cell-phone technology of the day, everyone had been informed eventually, and had arrived at a mostly empty parking lot by the beach only minutes after we did, midmorning on a weekday. Out we got. Onto the sand we went.

Our teacher wore robes, layers of them, and by the time he got down to a comfortable number of layers, it looked as though he was wearing an ankle-length maroon skirt under a sleeveless muscle T-shirt vest, trimmed in brocade. His attendants, young Westerners this time, were in their travel clothes—sport coats and pressed summer wool slacks. The several protectors wore their uniforms. Since it had been cold and windy in the early morning, I was in a heavy three-piece pinstripe wool suit, including the vest. Now, in the sun, it was broiling. We were all in our polished street shoes, except our teacher, who wore sandals.

When the teacher is on foot, especially in a city, the protectors like to surround him, though not too closely. Their various patterns necessarily deform and contract in crowds or at speed, but here on the open beach, with nothing but the North Sea to our left and grass-tufted dunes to our right, they could walk in a precise diamond. I dropped back to walk with the attendants. They, too, had flown through the night, and if they wore out, the whole visit would be more difficult. They also frequently had messages to convey; at the very least, they could give us a sense of how things had gone at the last stop, how the travel had been, the food, the health, the mood—anything. They were tremendously and admirably discreet, though. Until they knew you and trusted you, you got pretty much nothing.

For about ten minutes we went down the beach, meeting no one. We had fresh air, a breeze, exercise; it seemed ideal. Then we came upon a group of sunbathers, about five or six women distributed on beach towels. They propped themselves up on their elbows to gawk at us. They wore sun hats and dark glasses and lay otherwise naked to the sky, and now to our eyes. They did not appear to be shy. They must have wondered at us, walking in strange formation, wearing what must have looked like theater costumes. Our teacher surely spotted them—he misses very little—but he gave no sign. He did not alter his gait nor turn his head; nothing. We went on for another ten minutes or so, then turned back and had had exactly the same awkward, silent, curious encounter, except now they were on our left, instead of our right.

It had been all right: our teacher was not required to live as a celibate monk. Being suddenly confronted with six naked women posed no problem to his formal vows. In fact, we rather needed him to marry at some point and produce offspring, heirs.

With the monks in the VIP Lounge, and most certainly with His Holiness, this was very different. They were monks in the old, classical sense, and we could not intentionally put them in situations that increased the risk to their vows. Just getting them around Amsterdam had been hard enough. The van had been stopped in traffic more than once, with a canal on one side of the street and women (alas, very young ones too) nearly naked in windows on the other side. We'd had to sit there idling, looking at very little on the canal, until the cars had begun to move. So the beach was out. Besides, HH's legs were old and painful to him. He walked with difficulty, sometimes supported by monks left and right.

In any case, there wasn't a nice place we could sit and look at the sea—at least not at the beach we'd visited. A drafty snack bar with a slapping screen door and a cement roof was what we'd found before. Fries had been available, with mayo or ketchup. You could get coffee, tea, soda, candy, some old sandwiches, and praise the gods, beer. Given the hot walk in the three-piece suit, given the surprise change in plans, given the scenery at the beach, and some wrung-out nerves and the fact that I was not (as the protectors were) formally on duty, beer had been a real help. But beer would not help much this morning. If it helped anyone, it would be me, and my job now was not me; it was His Holiness, his attendant, and the nine monks.

There were surely other restaurants by the sea we could visit, or maybe museums, or perhaps another tour on the Amsterdam canals?—those had gone well. It would give them something to do while we developed alternative travel plans, or short-term, emergency, elegant hospitality. Paul and I approached His Holiness and his attendant. Goatee came over too. It felt like a baseball conference at the mound, except that Paul and I were squatted down in front of HH. Squatted down we stayed while they spoke among themselves in Tibetan. There were long pauses, bursts of words, grunts, noises of acknowledgement, pauses. They quizzed us about the possible flight in the afternoon, and we told them what little we knew. At one point, HH nodded in a simple, pronounced way to let Paul and me know they would now continue their discussion without us. We backed off uncertainly as they smiled, and continued nodding at us. Shortly, word came from the attendant that they would wait where they were. They would wait? They would wait. We cleared this with the airline staff, and began waiting.

As I said, one of the most impressive things about this Holiness was his stillness. Back at the centre, he'd rarely stirred from his room. It held a bed along one wall, with a nightstand next to it. There had been a large wingback chair, a table brought out for meals, a cabinet for hanging robes. There were mats for visitors. These were either spread on the floor bearing people, or stacked away. It wasn't spartan—a flower arrangements graced a corner, and one wall, made of sliding glass doors, gave onto a rock-moss garden with a very small pond. Though this was not classically Japanese, it was much more elegant than the views out the back lots of other houses in this block of town. But that was it: bed, chair, table, cabinet, view. HH had taken his meals in this room for ten days, conducted his business there, prepared the ceremonies. He seemed pleased with it, told us it was fine each time we asked, and we asked nearly every day. Sitting a day in the VIP Lounge would be nothing for him.

The other thing about His Holiness, possibly related to this first quality, was how, when he sat on his throne to lead a ceremony, he could bring it. I'd had the good fortune through the years to witness, or to participate in, quite a number of Tibetan Buddhist empowerments. Some had been restricted ceremonies, open only to initiates who'd proved themselves in preliminary practices; some had been large, public blessings. These had been led by a variety of teachers and lineage holders, and all had been good. Excellent. One is not to judge—particularly not with the usual small mind—how teachers had done, or how effective a ceremony had been. The transmissions, we were told, took place beyond self-oriented consciousness and were not something you could know or hold onto in a comparative way. Once the teachers ascended the ceremonial thrones, donned ceremonial clothing, chanted specific liturgy, and made ritual gestures, they entered a role transcending their daily personalities.

Still, there are qualities; one notices styles, characteristics. One teacher might enchant (literally) with voice; another might stop the collective mind of an assembly with incisive commentary. It might be impossible to look away from the graceful hand gestures of yet another. All of these things had happened to me. I'd been stilled by viewing a ceremonial crown, or the movements of long brocade sleeves, the flashing of jewel ornaments. With this Holiness, it was atmosphere. An hour or so into a morning's liturgy, I'd repeatedly noticed a charge seeming to permeate the room. The air had felt enriched, as though by uranium, I suppose; it had become thicker, but brighter, not duller. A thin mist of light. This perception was not mine alone; others felt it too. At lunch break in such a ceremony, my ex-wife mentioned how intense it had been in there. Some people I'd observed during the morning looking around, being distracted, whispering, giggling with a neighbor—even they might volunteer that the vibes had been *amazing*. Man! Couldn't WAIT for tomorrow.

I later learned that HH had been known for this in Asia as well, and that this intensification of the space had been identified in India millennia ago, and named. It had come across to English relatively recently as *blessing*. Despite his squarish silver glasses, and his blocky, unglamorous appearance, when he took the high seat and waved the blue woogie (as a one friend put it) His Holiness could absolutely bring the blessings.

A person of his physical durability, his stillness, his undeniable focus, and his shamanic abilities was not to be contradicted. Thus, when word came, maybe forty-five minutes later, that HH wished us all to leave the VIP Lounge, that is what we all did. He made clear he meant everyone in his party (except his attendant) and everyone in ours. The monks were divided into two groups; Paul and Goatee took one, and I was to take the other one, assisted by Titia, protector second-in-command. The idea was that we should go out and look around. By the door, I glanced back at HH, just to make sure, and he beamed a big smile, and nodded; he gestured outwardly with his large hand, as if gently shooing away flies. Paul and I agreed that his group would go right, and ours would go left, and we'd meet back in about an hour. This meant exiting the secure area, so we did a passport check.

I'd admired Titia earlier as she'd stood by the top of the outside stairs, and I could admire her all I wanted—she seemed to encourage this by dressing, even in uniform, in ways that flattered her—but for naught: she played for the other team. Earlier in life she'd skated for the Dutch Olympic team and she had maintained, if not competitive form, at least a distinct fitness. All that she'd skated with was still strong and shapely. Titia was usually in one difficult relationship or another—recently it had been with a long-haired older painter, beautiful in a red-blonde way one saw in old Dutch paintings. Titia wore her brown hair mannishly short, which seemed useful for interactions with the monks.

Off we went. Since we were passing time, we simply sauntered, pausing to look in shop windows. The monks tended to be most interested in electronics and gaming displays. Under their short hair and robes, parallel to their special training, they were, after all, young men—late teens to mid-twenties, I would have guessed, though it was hard to judge. We were definitely a group of people out of step with most of the airport's population, who streamed hurriedly around us. Several times we had to flatten ourselves along the edges of the hall to make room for flashing, beeping, aggressively driven motorized carts carrying the infirm and elderly. When we had done the shops up one side of the terminal and back down the other, we went up a level to the observation deck and took tea in one of the restaurants there.

Out on the balcony, the monks seemed to dislike being in direct sunlight, whenever it broke through the clouds. They shielded themselves against it, draping their outer robe over a raised arm. Some wrapped their heads in their outer robe, using it like a long scarf. Otherwise they seemed pleased to watch the variety of airplanes taxiing about, taking off, and landing. It did not feel particularly scenic up there, though with land as flat as this was, you could see quite a distance. As usual in the Netherlands, some body of water or another was nearby. The sky and the stunning light all around reminded me how this country had produced a long string of remarkable painters, especially landscape painters.

After a leisurely period of looking, we dawdled back, and as we'd hoped to do, we met the other group. It wasn't much past midday. We debated going back into the VIP Lounge for lunch snacks, but were discouraged from this by having to clear security again—and more deeply, by not really having understood His Holiness's wish. Did he send the monks and us out because he thought we'd enjoy it, or had he done so to ensure a higher degree of peace and quiet in the VIP Lounge? We'd had tea only a while ago, so our group, at least, was good to do the side of the airport we hadn't yet seen.

Paul told how Goatee had gone into a couple of jewelry

stores looking for eight-sided crystals. This being a diamond capital, he'd been told he could easily have such a thing made. How long would the gentleman be in town? In which sort of price range was he looking? Scanning other prices in the shops, Goatee had demurred, then declined any purchase. This second side of the terminal was longer, and had more shops than the side we'd just seen—including some of the same shops. The monks were infallibly gentle, and at least pretended an interest in the windows, though we had to scurry past an erotic shop, with its frank display of adult toys, video box covers, and lingerie on overly endowed mannequins. Not for the first time, I experienced an odd phenomenon: how the shops and restaurants seemed so magnetizing when you were rushing past them; but how, if you were condemned to wait some hours and you walked around and inspected these places, they lost their glamour. The goods revealed themselves to be cheaply made, repetitive, and overpriced. The shrugging boredom of the staff replaced the seduction and delight that came—perhaps only imaginarily—with a quick or passing glance.

In one of the large chain newsstands I bought two American newspapers. Normally I would have spent a great deal more time in the bookshop, flipping through magazines, rummaging among the English-language books for anything I hadn't read. With monks along, however, a newsstand visit had to be brief. There was much in the place—even the covers of the paperbacks or magazines—that did not conform to monastic standards. In the panoramic restaurant on this side, I again invited everyone to tea and a snack, checking first that I had enough guilders.

Midafternoon we went through the various checks required

to reenter the VIP Lounge, and found that Paul's group had already returned. Judging from their casual postures, it seemed that HH was fine with everyone being there. The short, bouncy monk had somehow worn out completely, and now lay fully reclined on a couch, with an arm up behind his head, staring at the ceiling. I couldn't remember ever seeing a monk so disposed, especially in the proximity of the teacher. The others, though, paid him no attention—they seemed to think nothing of it. If they weren't completely or partially horizontal themselves, they were at this hour no longer able to conceal their boredom. HH seemed exactly as we'd left him: settled, calmly cheerful on his couch, with his attendant in a nearby chair.

The airline people busied themselves with screens and forms, standing behind their little podia. They'd told Paul the likelihood of an afternoon flight had increased, and they would soon know for certain. The lounge contained some other passengers now— several Chinese businessmen sat in a cluster in a distant corner, and a couple of tall Southern Europeans also talked nearby. They looked peaked, tired. The television sets suspended around the lounge were on, and just loud enough to make it hard to hear, or overhear, them. Eventually I picked up that they were Spanish. Someone had thoughtfully put a little TV on the round table next to HH's couch. The sound was muted, and the set had been turned outward so that HH did not have to look at the incessant imagery. I gave Paul one of my newspapers, then saw a stack of complimentary copies now sitting in the racks near the toilets: Dutch, American, and English.

Restraining my impulse to turn straight to the sports section, I dutifully began working through some of the main international stories, though I suspected that with the general level of distraction and fatigue, I wouldn't get far. True enough, ·I was roused from deeply nodding off by a gentle tap on the shoulder from Goatee. As my context came back into place, the words Goatee said began to make sense, even if they remained puzzling. His Holiness would like to speak with me. Right now? Right now, please.

On my way across the lounge, Paul and the jacketless agent converged to say that a flight would be going to Greece this afternoon, after all. They'd begin boarding in about a half hour. Buoyed by this, I approached HH as respectfully as I could, slowing my pace as I neared him, bowing my head, inclining my body, and then kneeling in front of him. His attendant had joined HH on the couch. I asked if everything was OK and relayed the news about the flight and the timing. As the attendant translated, HH showed no emotion, nor any surprise. He said a few guttural words in Tibetan and Goatee, who'd been loitering nearby, went off to ready the monks. Paul had come with me, all but the last few paces, and he now walked off to certify with the other protectors and the airline that the luggage was where it was supposed to be.

Kneeling there in front of HH as this bit of commotion took place, I felt my eyes being drawn to the little TV on his side table. It was not quite at eye level, but it was much closer to my head than His Holiness's head was, and it was facing me. HH's squint seemed as much chosen to repel attention as to meet it, while this television, like all televisions, used every trick to draw your eye.

Not that I was a hard catch. I'd grown up sitting hours per day in front of a set. It hadn't been on at meals (which were taken in a dining room) nor had I let it play during study time. But for certain shows, or news, or important political speeches, TV viewing had been a family event. Saturday morning we children parked in front of the set for cartoons, largely ignoring adults, who would look in every half hour or so to scold that we were mesmerized. Surely we were. Males watched sports weekend afternoons; this was simply understood, very rarely contravened: the cause would have to be a funeral or other family obligation— or a religious observance that could not be gotten around. Only as a grown-up myself, and only with struggle, had I been able to develop the strength to look away from a TV screen, or any screen, regardless of what was on. Like a rude guest at a party, these pictures dominate your attention, I'd had to tell myself. They won't let you alone.

At present, to my simultaneous delight and horror, what was being shown on HH's little set was baseball. How could this be? For the several years I'd lived in Europe I'd never found baseball, and not for lack of trying. Once in a rare while, on military radio they might broadcast a game between two teams I didn't care about. Late on Sunday nights you could find American football, the games condensed and punctuated with graphic advertisements for phone sex. Basketball could be found. Baseball? Never. Yet here it was, with my beloved San Francisco Giants at bat. I'd bought the newspaper partly to see how they were doing in their bitter fight with the New York Mets for the National League championship. The winner would advance to the World Series. I hadn't seen a game all season, yet here, kneeling on the floor of the VIP Lounge, on a late afternoon in Schiphol Airport in Amsterdam, I could watch. Except that I really, really couldn't. I managed to yank my eyes off the screen in time to meet HH's gaze as it returned to me, having finished speaking to his attendant. They both looked at me now, with some playful feeling, as if I were a new pledge in a fraternity. They were senior members.

Holiness would like to know, began the attendant, if you have ever seen a ghost.

What? Excuse me? Have I ever—seen a ghost?

The attendant looked up, as if consulting a bilingual dictionary written in air. Ghost, he said. Yes, I think that's the right word. Ghost. Ghost.

HH smiled broadly in his seat. I tried to think if I'd ever seen a ghost, but all that came to mind were questions. Why is he asking me this? Why now? He's been here ten days; I've seen him every day. It had specifically been my job not to chatter with him, nor to talk about myself in any way. In our meetings we'd gone over the schedule, the logistics, the plans, the people, then I'd gotten gone. Now, with him a few minutes from boarding a plane, with the Giants in trouble a couple of feet from my unruly eyes, he wants to talk about ghosts?

It flitted through my mind that he was being kind. Perhaps with everything behind us, having gone reasonably well, and even departure now seemingly assured, this conversation was a kind of reward?—a personal moment, a chance to open up with His Holiness?

I think I've seen a ghost—or ghosts—I'm not sure, I said, and waited while the attendant translated. I thought I might have a second to check the TV, but HH's eyebrows rose up as he listened. I could see more of his eyes than I ever had, and they were looking at me.

Holiness would like to know what happened. When referring

to HH, his attendant tended to drop the "His." I related, in sections I hoped the attendant would be able to remember and translate, the story of what had occurred one chilly autumn night in the mountains of California, when I'd been a young resident in a monastery. I'd climbed to my cabin, one of three along a ridge, built with a shared bathroom on a small plateau, before the hill continued up increasingly steeply, becoming a sheer cliff at the top. That night, I'd gotten ready for bed, crawled into my sleeping bag, and extinguished the kerosene lantern. Almost immediately, it seemed, I'd heard a strong buzzing sound, mixed with gruff male voices. I'd definitely felt the presence of other beings around me. The message coming from the voices—or from somewhere— was an invitation: I should go with them. I remember thinking, Why not? I'm invited, I should go. I started. Then I panicked and pulled back. With what felt like enormous effort, I'd pulled myself out and awakened, gasping for air and drenched with sweat. Then I'd gotten out of bed and, with a flashlight, made my way to the bathroom cabin, shaking and panting in the night air. Eventually I went back to bed and lay there, heart pounding, until sleep came. This is all I told HH.

Back at the monastery the next day, I had told the story to a friend on my work crew, and she'd advised me to tell the Abbot. She'd told the Abbot herself, in fact, and soon enough an interview had been arranged. There, I told the whole thing again. After a long pause, the Abbot's response had been to ask if I'd ever read the *Tibetan Book of the Dead*. This had not been comforting. He'd explained that the point of the book was how to relate to such phenomena when they occurred. He said that when one did intense practice, as we were doing, particularly isolated in the mountains, as we were, such things could happen. One was supposed to relate with them as emanations of mind. However frightening or real such things seemed, they were not apart from our own fundamental being, our own mind. The point was to see them like that. Obviously, I didn't go in to any of this with HH. I'm not sure I even remembered it at the moment, since I hadn't told the story in thirty years. And he knew it anyway, of course.

The attendant passed along all that I did say to HH, and they had a little discussion. As they spoke with each other, my eyes slid toward the screen. It felt as if I were dragging huge iron rollers to bring them back forward, where I knew they should be. I could read about the damn game, I scolded myself inwardly. I'm talking with His Holiness! But my face was surely contorted with effort when the attendant addressed me. He smiled briefly. Holiness says he knows about that class of beings, he began. HH wore his broadest smile ever, and it appeared that his shoulders were shaking up and down slightly, as if suppressing laughter. Holiness says they *are* a kind of ghost. They like to live in high, narrow places. The attendant and HH were gesturing above their heads, describing chimney-like shapes with their hands. They have them sometimes in Tibet. They can be little dangerous.

So it was good I didn't go with them? I asked. I wondered if HH actually needed all the translation, because in response to this he said something right away, before the attendant had started to speak.

Holiness says everything OK.

The young airline man came, wearing his jacket this time and pushing a wheelchair. If His Holiness would like to board now…? A general commotion ensued. I got the scarf ready again, and we gathered by the exit of the VIP Lounge to bid His Holiness and then the entire party farewell.

They made it to Greece just fine, we learned, together with all their luggage. The Giants lost that game, and eventually they lost the series.

Beautiful Writing

id you say *spinach* or *Spanish*?

They were riding in the back of a car. She took so long to answer that he began to wonder if he should ask again. Maybe it would be better to just swallow it, pretend he hadn't spoken.

I said both, she said at last. I said I'd eaten a spinach omelet in a Spanish restaurant. Only it wasn't called an omelet. It was called a tortilla, and that was confusing. It was this enormous *thing*, filling the whole plate—full of fried onions and potatoes and spinach, all baked with egg. There was egg all through it. This was a Spanish place, not a Mexican place. It sat there my plate, defying me to eat it. I ate it, too—most of it. It tasted good, but it was so large that I needed some sauce to go with it, and a number of glasses of wine to get it down.

Hot sauce?

She nodded. I asked for hot sauce, and he brought me a dish of something green, and told me that this what usually went with a tortilla. It seemed to be a creamed garlic, or a garlic mayonnaise. What I said before was that because of a spinach omelet, I'd had

113

restless dreams and slept badly. Maybe it was the raw garlic, or the wine. Or maybe it was all just too much. Anyway, I couldn't fall asleep until this morning, and then I overslept.

Her recital of the meal this time contained enough new details to cause Andrea, in the front passenger seat, to twist around and look at Shelly while she spoke. Andrea nodded to encourage her, but said nothing. Shelly used her hands in the telling. She showed the shape of the omelet—like a pie—and its dimensions, also like a store-bought family-sized pie. She fluttered her hands and fingers around her head, to signify the restless thoughts that had kept her awake and made her late.

Grady had not paid much attention the first time she'd told this, because he'd been trying to do something else. He'd gotten out of the car while they all had waited for Shelly to emerge from the house. Upon arrival, Andrea and her husband, Andrew, had consulted about the address, and Andrea had finally gone up on the porch and rung the bell. It turned out to be the right place, but the news was that Shelly would be a little while. So Grady walked with slow steps up and down the street, not going far from the car. This section of Oakland could be dangerous, though the particular block of small houses looked OK. It was also early in the morning. As he walked, Grady began mentally to recite the chants he'd had to skip in order to catch the train over here. When he got further from the car he murmured the words aloud; as he got closer, he recited silently. They'd be doing them about now back at the center, he thought. He was most of the way through when Shelly came onto the porch with a man helping to carry her luggage. Grady lost his place.

The man was good-looking, not tall, wearing a knit vest

open over the brown skin of his torso. His muscles were sharply defined, and they slid easily over one another as he lifted the suitcase and rearranged things in the trunk. There had been brief smiles during the introductions. Waverly. Grady primarily noted Waverly's spherical Afro. It looked as if Shelly's hair, too, had been done at one point into a spherical bowl of curls, but being dark-blonde and thin, it had not held very tightly.

Back in the car, Grady had closed his eyes and leaned against the door on his side, pretending to doze while he tried to finish the chants, and to recite a few other mantras and spells he thought might protect travelers. He'd come across these in the course of study; ancient Buddhist pilgrims from China to India recorded the supplications they'd made to deities, asking for protection on the long routes. Japanese voyagers on the shorter trip to China had done the same thing, especially when caught in rough seas.

This trip wasn't officially a pilgrimage, though Grady felt his intentions were virtuous. They were driving up from San Francisco Bay to the Columbia Gorge, there to take part in an annual calligraphy conference, with one of the most venerable teachers in the country, a founder of the modern calligraphic revival. Grady knew the teacher, whom everyone simply called Lars, from his own years at college. He had also gone hiking many times in Columbia Gorge, but he'd never been to the place they were going. They were to stay in a lodge built in the early twentieth century by members of a mystic Christian group. It was supposed to be perfect for conferences, with a mixture of private rooms and public spaces. Several hiking trails originated from it. The lodge was built on what was reputed to be a magical location, a power spot.

Is Shelly a nickname? Andrea asked. Are you really a Rochelle or a Michelle or something?

No, Shelly replied, covering an enormous yawn with one hand, and holding up the other to signal she had more to say. She squeezed her eyes shut and popped them open a few times. She shook her head. My mother apparently liked this singer—or actress, I'm a little vague on it. Anyway, she named me Shelly after her. I think I'm going to doze. Do you mind?

She pulled a jacket over herself, closed her eyes, leaned against the door, and went to sleep. Soon, though, she'd shifted away from the door, and slept centered in her seat, with her head straight back and her mouth open. After that, her head flopped forward. It wobbled with curves in the road, lane changes, and bumps. From the front seat, Andrea cast repeated worried glances back at Shelly, then over at Andrew, then forward out the front windshield. She finally signaled to Grady to move to the middle seat. He unharnessed himself and slid left. Without obviously waking, Shelly immediately turned in her seatbelt, put her head on Grady's shoulder, and fitted the rest of her body against his. Surprisingly near, he thought. There was a lot of her up against him as she seemed to descend deeper into sleep.

They stayed more or less like this, the car quiet, as they drove long, flat stretches up the Central Valley toward Oregon. At last the road started to climb from the plain and to bank left and right. The air smelled less baked in the bursts of it that Andrew let into the car. Mount Shasta appeared, unbelievable even in glimpses, until as they got closer they could see its full magnificence, ruling the hundreds of miles of landscape from which it rose. They stopped for fuel and lunch in the small town associated with it.

Shelly emerged from the car wobbly, startled by the dramatic shift in scenery.

Being on its foot made it hard to see the scale of the mountain, though Grady felt force, or forces, emanating from it. Despite its striking symmetry against the land and sky, it seemed to him there was more than visual beauty. It wasn't exactly aural, though he was sure that if he were more sensitive, he would be able to hear the mountain as well. Whatever it was, he felt he was picking up a sort of message, and the radiance did not seem completely benevolent. Not quite a threat, but maybe a kind of warning.

They read on the restaurant placemats some of the gaudier legends—how people and things had simply disappeared on the mountain; how it was reputed to be a kind of mystic zone. Andrew had picked up a selection of giveaway flyers from a rack by the cash register, and in one of these they learned about the veneration with which Native Americans had approached the power spots and indeed the entire area. Another flyer told how the mountain had, with an avalanche and a fire, seemingly shaken off a ski resort under construction in the 1930s. Their waitress, observing them reading, told them there was much more literature about the mountain in the two bookstores up in town. One featured camping-type books: the trails, flora, fauna, rock-climbing, cycling; the other store leaned toward legends, ghost stories, and spiritual vibrations—including tales about the kingdom inside the mountain,. You had to visit both stores, she said. Over a BLT on white toast, Grady resolved that he would come back and do just that.

Up in Oregon, the road again flattened and straightened. The scenery verged on monotonous, though it was very green. They drove in and out of pockets of rain, under a darkening afternoon sky. Shelly did not even pretend sociability, though she did ask Grady if she might stretch out across the back seat. She didn't have to point out that this meant resting her head on his thigh, using it as a pillow; it was obvious to both of them. It was only her ear and the blonde curls of her head, but it meant a steady pressure down there. They shifted a few times to get settled, then Shelly slipped back off to sleep. Grady tried to pretend to Andrea and Andrew, and to himself as well, that this was normal, something that happened all the time—that a young, attractive stranger laid her head in his lap. He tried to remember her body, now wrapped up under her jacket and a cover, and found that all too easily he could. She possessed a tomboy energy coming off the porch this morning, and she stood in what seemed to be a slightly competitive slouch. She'd led with her pelvis. Grady found that these reflections were not helping him, and tried to direct his mind elsewhere.

The misty air out the window—part precipitation, part road spray—made him think of times he'd stood along this very highway hitchhiking between school in Portland and Zen in San Francisco. It had mostly been all right, though there had been frightening misadventures as well. One occurred near where they were now, in southern Oregon. Grady and his hitching partner Gene had stood on the apron of the highway for a couple of cold hours, until at dusk, a pickup truck had finally pulled off the road for them, they thought. They'd barely noticed in time that the approaching headlights were not slowing, and they'd been forced to dive into the brambles bordering the road. Through dust hanging in the air, from the cab of the truck they'd heard raucous laughter, and they'd watched as a couple of empty beer cans came flying out the side window. Unpleasant though it had been, the incident had at least been brief and impersonal.

Much creepier had been the time when three rurals picked them up in Northern California, and without warning or explanation, taken a series of exits leading to a hilly dirt road with no traffic on it. The talk had turned malevolent, against faggots (which Grady, at least, was not—he had no idea about Gene) and against long-haired hippie types, which both of them were. Ax handles had appeared from a work box in the front seat, and it seemed clear to Grady that he and Gene were in for a beating, at least. They'd tried to talk their way out of it, and had finally offered the roughs some weed as ransom. Fortunately, one fat joint sat already rolled in their stash. Very soon, the front seat was high. Either from a change of heart, or from rowdy distraction, the violent plan had faded. Grady and Gene, after enduring more verbal abuse, had been let go not far from the freeway. They'd made their way as quickly as possible to the bus station. Even to think of it now, ten years later, made Grady uneasy. That had been his last time hitchhiking. Life in a meditation center, and Buddhism's strictures against intoxication, meant that marijuana had also gone out of his life long ago. Teachers of the day had weaned their hippie students off it. Whatever effects cannabis might or might not have, Grady knew that at least this once, that plant and its powers had saved his bones.

Shelly yawned and shifted, and lay for a while on her back. Not long after that, she turned onto her left side. This meant she was facing Grady rather than the front seat. Facing, thought Grady, could be the name of a sexual act. If she drooled in her sleep—this seemed possible because of her presently open mouth—it would later look as if he had wet his pants. Least of my worries, he told himself; I'm wearing black pants. To think further about Shelly or the disposition of her body, to think further about the fact that there were just a couple of layers of cotton cloth between her lips and his skin—these could only lead to a state of heightened frustration.

He tried again to think of other things. There wasn't much out the window beyond dark fields, and behind them woods, streaked over from time to time with orange as Andrea flicked cigarette ash out her side. Through the front, he could see a row of taillights, cut by windshield wipers refreshing the view every second or so. He didn't want to drive mentally, so he closed his eyes and tried to remember his college days in Portland, and especially the excursions he'd made to the Columbia Gorge.

These had only been possible when someone from his dorm was driving and his homework load was light. If only he hadn't been so stoned all the time, he thought, he might have sharper memories. But as he brought his mind repeatedly back to the outings, and away from the warmth of Shelly's light snoring at the joint of his legs, details began to emerge: the van they'd mostly used for these trips, how he'd sat on the carpeted floor of it, how it had rocked from side to side, despite the relaxed driving style of—Larry, was it? from somewhere in the South. Alabama? With a mustache. Not only had the roads been curvy, but the gusts coming down the Gorge had buffeted the van so hard it had seemed to ride briefly on two wheels. He remembered the immense river and the stark bluffs along it, and his initial resistance when Larry would finally slide open the side door of the van and everyone would sit there lacing up boots in the parking lot. Was it pure imagination, he wondered, that he could now again feel the sudden clarity brought by cool air, or by the penetrating smell of laurel and pine? Did it matter that he was recalling things from the past—did it make them less real?

What was real, anyway? They had been discussing this just the other night in a class on Buddhist philosophy at the center— about how Buddha had posited early on that perception was part of mind, indivisible from mind, and that there were implications of that. The cool thing, Grady thought, was that Buddhists had subsequently disagreed about the qualities of this mind, and fought about it, and developed real schools of practice and study that differed from one another. There had been passionate debates, temporary winners and losers. As Buddhism spread to other lands, one or another of the schools had dominated, and influenced the national view. The teacher of Grady's class had reached into Western philosophy—as he so easily could, and so often did—to point out that similar debates had broken out in eighteenth-century England among the philosophers. Particularly he'd cited Bishop Berkeley, and his theories that perception was based on the mind's memory, and that what we knew as the world was basically thought. He'd gone on to tell how another great thinker—Johnson, wasn't it?—had not liked this, and in a challenge, had stepped onto a beach and kicked a rock with all his force. He'd then declared—no doubt hopping about on one leg—I refute thee THUS, Bishop Berkeley. The class had laughed and moved on, but the question about what is real remained. Maybe this girl, dozing in his lap, was Johnson's rock, Grady thought. Mental construct or not, she seemed to be very much there. She was a problem.

The house where Grady—and it turned out Shelly as well—were to spend the night was in a section of Portland he didn't know. His school sat in the southeast, and almost all his time had been spent there, with brief forays across the river to visit Chinese restaurants. Those outings had taken place in the dark, and had required a car. He hadn't paid much attention to where they'd gone. The city mapped itself into quadrants, and had been laid out with a generous sense of space: long, straight avenues, room for parks, street trees, yards front and back. On some of its borders Portland melted almost seamlessly into farmland. The house they were to stay in tonight belonged to a college friend of Andrea's who'd agree to put up a couple of people for the night. The plan was that they'd leave Portland late morning, and head up the Gorge. Andrew and Andrea were staying elsewhere.

There had been warm greetings, and a bit of conversation, but with respect for everyone's obvious fatigue, Grady and Shelly were rather quickly deposited with their bags. The house's owner, a solidly built woman, had been waiting, she told them, and she needed to leave soon. Here was the room, there was the bathroom. The kitchen was downstairs in the back, but there was a coffee shop on the corner. Here was a key, and a telephone number where she could be reached in an emergency. She'd either be back late tonight or tomorrow morning; good evening. Perhaps it was that she wore a dark-blue suit with white edging, but something in her manner struck Grady as military.

Their room, clearly occupied by a young person once, held a bed, a dark-green, puffy sofa, a desk, and some standing lamps. It also served these days as a storage space, and perhaps a studio. Paintings of several sizes leaned against one wall, facing away, so that only the pine stretchers on the back were visible. An easel stood in the corner. Toolboxes sat in front of the paintings, some closed, some not. In the open ones, tubes of color writhed over one another. Jam jars held desiccated remnants of fluid.

They set their bags down, Shelly by the bed, Grady by the big couch. After riffling briefly through her things, Shelly pulled out a towel and went off without comment to the bathroom. Grady tested the couch by sitting on it. Firm enough; also long enough and probably wide enough, though convex and a bit dusty. In his sleeping bag, which he now opened to air, he thought he'd be fine. Having done nothing but sit all day in a car, he felt oddly fatigued. He sat for days at a stretch in the center, he thought, but not slouched in a car seat, and not with a constant dose of secondhand cigarette smoke. At the center, he sat in an airy hall: his posture was better, there were breaks, and there was nothing in his lap except his own feet, his robes, and his hands in the gesture of meditation. There was no conversation, and on lucky days, less distracted thinking.

A walk around one of Portland's long blocks would surely do him good, he thought, but as he looked out past the single white curtain, he realized that the hushed sound he'd been unconsciously hearing was rain. It came down steadily; he wouldn't be able to pretend it wasn't happening, as he'd so often done before. He sat wondering how he could have come to Portland without an umbrella, when Shelly returned to the room wrapped in two towels; one on her head and one around her body. She drew a horizontal circle in the air with her index finger, as though stirring something. Grady turned around. Neither spoke until she said OK. He saw her then dressed in a silk bathrobe that descended to the middle of her thighs. She was working out where to hang her towel, where to air her clothes.

How's the bathroom?

It's OK. It's fine, she said, without looking away from what she was doing. How's this room?

Kind of crowded but OK. A lot of stuff.

When Grady returned to the bedroom, he set his travel kit down on his sleeping bag, and hung a washcloth across the lower lip of the easel. Sitting on the side of the bed, Shelly attended to her fingernails.

You weren't planning to sleep over there, were you? I mean, it's kind of small, but I think we can both fit in this bed. If that's OK. It'll be warmer. She looked up and patted the cover beside her, as she might have done to invite a pet, and Grady approached with all the forethought and restraint of a tail-wagging puppy.

This was as much discussion as they had. Within seconds they were kissing, and very shortly after that, Shelly's bathrobe was out of the way, and Grady was on the bed in his underpants. These Shelly removed from him, pulling them unhurriedly toward his feet. He lifted his hips to make sure nothing obstructed her. Then she lay as she had in the afternoon, recapitulating positions from the back seat—her head on the top of his thighs, not doing anything apart from breathing on him. Finally she began.

They went on for a couple of hours, almost without speaking. There seemed no need; their bodies, perhaps from so much contact in the car, were at ease, able to match the other's shapes and pulses without talk. They did make noises of pleasure. Shelly seemed fully restored from her long sleep in the car, and she repeatedly roused Grady to match her energy. Neither of them mentioned Waverly, though Grady thought of him a few times. The dangers of unprotected sex were not unknown to them— newspapers were full of the topic—but it was not something either of them brought up. By timely withdrawal Grady at least dealt with the risk of impregnation, though Shelly told him, as he lay next to her catching his breath, that he need not have worried; she was on the pill. It would have been OK. About forty-five minutes later, he tested this; it seemed more than OK.

When he awoke Grady listened for rain, but heard none. The curtain over the window glowed white. His body felt sore, as if after sport, and he recalled that Shelly, for all her ability to meld her body to his, also had something of a wrestler in her. When she wanted a particular position, she had simply put Grady into it, sometimes forcefully. Her peaks of pleasure had been accompanied with percussive pushing—a kind of open-palm-heel-of-the-hand hitting, especially if she was above him. It had seemed fine at the time, and even now the aches were partly pleasurable. He shifted in the bed to climb out, and Shelly awoke. They discussed their sleep in the narrow bed. Grady had apparently sunk nearly instantly into dreams, while Shelly had lain awake, jostling him and repositioning him if he snored.

Do you think she's here?

I don't know. I didn't hear her come in.

I'd better wear something to the bathroom.

Shelly watched him, seeing his body for the first time in good light as he scrounged around for his underpants. He couldn't find them, so he just pulled on pants. She remained attentive as he tried to dress balancing first on one foot, then on the other. He second foot caught on something in the pant leg. He thought the cloth was just folded and would give way with more force, but as he pushed harder—still holding the waist of the pants—he managed to jerk himself off balance. With only unfamiliar furniture to brace him, he crashed to the floor, letting go of the pants just in time for his hands to smack the boards an instant before his upper body did. He had basically pulled himself into a nose dive.

Shelly found this hilarious and burst into laughter. Her peals were divided by gasping, and Grady realized how similar her gasps sounded to the wild breaths she took during sex. He heard her as he made his way to the bathroom, and as he returned to the room. He found her there wiping tears of laughter from her eyes. Aroused by her noise, he took off his pants and approached the bed, his intentions obvious.

Despite the relaxed pickup time, they nearly made themselves late with renewed pleasure, with leisurely showers, packing up, and breakfast at the local place. Still leery of eggs after the Spanish tortilla, Shelly had contented herself with coffee and toast. Grady ordered steak and eggs. She'd watched and then looked away as he put a steak sauce on the meat, hot sauce on the eggs, and ketchup on the potatoes. Later, he covered toast with butter and jam. I know, he said. Sorry—I'm a condiment freak. But it's all sitting right here on the table. We never get this stuff at the center.

It felt good to have eaten a solid meal as they walked back to the house and loaded their things into Andrew and Andrea's car. But as the trip took them from broad freeways to increasingly narrow and winding roads along the Columbia, Grady began to regret his breakfast. Only by keeping his gaze trained on far bluffs or distant clouds was he able to ward off car sickness. The monumental scenery helped; the constant gusting of wind did not.

I think I need to get out for a couple of minutes, he finally announced.

There's a place right up ahead, Andrea said. A scenic lookout.

Somehow, the sound of the word *lookout* made Grady feel even sicker, but it was indeed only a bit further until Andrew turned into a spacious parking lot and slowed. These were miserable, closed-eye minutes for Grady, who rolled his window all the way down as soon as they stopped. At first, everyone sat looking at the huge river coming through the land. The water roared as it moved, though it was impossible to untangle the sound of the river from the howl of the wind. Above, the sky was clear. Mist off the river and spray floating in the Gorge caught sunlight, and brightened the air with fragments of rainbows.

Never miss a chance, I always say, Andrew said, starting to open his door. Other people moving in the parking lot made the business of getting out of the car seem simple, though it was not. Wind put serious pressure on the car doors. When more than one door of a car was open, the wind came in and rattled things around. They had to move quickly to get out. Once standing, Grady leaned into the wind, supported by it. He felt again, as he had years earlier, overwhelmed by the scale of the view. There seemed no way to relate to it. His mind seemed too small; he could not comprehend the picture, nor relax with it. An appropriate response might be to compose a hymn for a church organ, or a symphony. He looked at the others and saw that they were happy, though their hair blew crazily, their eyes teared, their noses dripped. Andrew clamped a hand on his hat. Shelly and

Andrea leaned their heads together and appeared to be talking. Only a few feet away, Grady could not hear them.

Perhaps to signal that he felt better—he wasn't really sure why he did it—he suddenly jumped into the air. He held open the sides of his leather jacket like a flasher, and whooped as loudly as he could. The next thing he knew, he was looking up from the asphalt, about ten yards behind the car. He saw the faces of Andrea and Shelly as they bent over him, clutching their jackets closed. Andrea looked concerned. Shelly was laughing hard, for the second time that day, as he lay prostrate. The wind had caught his jacket like wings and batted him backward. The word *pterodactyl* came to mind. He had apparently been airborne briefly, and then, stumbling, been flattened onto his back. He'd clonked his skull. A watch cap he wore over his shaved head had softened the blow, but it had been enough to put him out for a couple of seconds. At least his short flight had not resulted in crashing into anything or anyone else, nor put him in the path of a moving car. He felt a number of things, but carsick was no longer one of them.

They arrived at the retreat center in early afternoon, without further incident. Among the several outbuildings, Andrea and Andrew occupied a private double room. Shelly had been sent to a six-bed dorm, and Grady found he'd been posted to a room with two single beds, and that he was the first to arrive. Word was that women usually outnumbered men roughly two to one at these retreats.

He took his few supplies to the central hall, where tables stood on folded-out legs, and he claimed a place at the end of one of them. Floor-to-ceiling windows bordered the open space, and a skylight had been cut into the ceiling. Several participants had already arranged their materials and workspaces. They'd propped up pieces of wood to form inclined writing surfaces, and they'd clamped desk lamps to table edges. At several seats, tackle boxes sat open to reveal layers of writing materials. Grady had only brought a single wooden box, though it was an heirloom from his grandparents. It had probably held cigars or other tobacco in its day, a day that began in the nineteenth century in a wealthy household in Turkey, he'd been told. Elaborate inlays of mica, mother-of-pearl, and other shiny flaked stones covered the lid, outside and in. This top had been hinged to a lined base and provided exactly the depth he needed for ink bottles. There was room enough for replacement pens—nibs and barrels—some rulers, and a protractor. He'd filled the remaining space with soft cloth, then wrapped the whole box in a square piece of Japanese printed cotton. This he'd tied so that the four corners met in a topknot.

Judging from the array of pillows and blankets strewn on the chairs, Grady thought that the calligraphers here must be as particular, and as dedicated to comfort, as meditators back at the center. Nothing he saw surprised him. His own setup back home was an inclined drafting table with a lamp clamped to it. The chair he sat on there held a pillow to adjust his height, and a blanket to drape over his legs. Given the extreme slowness of the work, the silence, the aloneness, several modern masters had spoken of calligraphy as a kind of meditation in action, a view Grady shared. Historically, the art had been nurtured by spiritual communities. Sacred manuscripts, Books of Hours, illuminated pages, and the importance of the scriptoria in monasteries both Eastern and Western testified to this.

On the other hand, some argued that writing was a degeneration from the oral and mnemonic traditions, pointing to its crudeness as compared to mind-to-mind transmissions of wisdom. Maybe so, mused Grady as he untied his bundle. Maybe it really was all about how many cows and sheep, or how many slaves were traded and for what, or how many had been killed in the last battle, and who now ruled what stretch of land. Humans had certainly done all that, and were doing it still. But it was hard to square this with the fact that early writing systems were nearly universally seen as of divine origin, as gifts from the gods.

Whatever the origin, once handwriting had coupled with religious practice, it issued a number of beautiful offspring: the tradition of sacred letters and mystical signs, for example, in which a character took on secret meaning in itself, additional to whatever other functions is fulfilled in the script. Such glyphs had long fascinated Grady, who'd seen them while looking at early Sanskrit writing, and seen them again in illuminated medieval Western manuscripts, as the Chi-Rho pages of Gospels. The disciplines of sitting to copy out religious texts, decorating them, binding them into books—these were other examples, necessary to the continuation of religion at first, and after printing arrived, sources of virtuous contemplation and the accumulation of merit.

The project Grady had brought to the retreat came from this tradition. He planned to continue copying out one of the Buddhist sutras that, along with its practical message of detachment and compassion, its philosophy of emptiness and interconnection, contained emphatic advice that a devotee should learn the text by heart, copy it by hand, explain it to others, extol it, venerate it, and generally see to its propagation. Grady understood that he was only the latest in a long line of scribes, monks, and laypeople who'd taken these encouragements to heart. The hour of copying he scraped from his day made no logical sense to him, and he was dreadfully slow at it, completing only two or three lines in a sitting. But when he managed to get himself in place, with paper ruled and his hand warmed up—when he actually put pen to paper—it felt addictively satisfying. He mentally criticized the letters as they appeared, and he worried over errors he might make in spelling or punctuation, but whenever he finished a session he felt—what was the word—good? right? complete? As if he had at least done *something* with that day. A day with sutra copying in it was a good day. Sometimes he thought that if there were no other reward to it than that, it was enough to bring him back to the table.

Is that your place? You're sitting there? Shelly asked. We're on the other side. Come see.

He followed Shelly and Andrea through the thicket of tables and chairs to their seats, which, Shelly explained, they'd chosen to in order to profit from natural light. Andrea seemed to know everyone; she stopped or was stopped so frequently that Shelly and Grady walked on ahead without her.

You know people here?

Some, she said. I came once a couple of years ago. How's your room?

I'm in a double, but the other guy's not here yet. Yours?

Two other women so far. It's OK. They're nice.

After determining they had an hour until cocktail time, they ran out of things to talk about.

You want to take a little walk? The grounds are pretty, and there are some spectacular views.

They went out sliding doors to a wooden deck, and followed a plank extension of it to its end. Come on, Shelly urged, descending the couple of steps to a path. They followed this past plantings of shrubs and some construction works. That path, she said at a junction, goes to one of the real hiking trails. If we go along it a bit, we'll see the river.

They walked through the trees, and Grady felt, as he often did in nature, that he should know more plant names. They moved through a mixed forest he knew, with both conifers and broadleaf deciduous trees, but if these were beech, or ash, or some kind of oak, or another species entirely, he had no idea. The damp air held pockets of fragrance, some of them sharp and slightly medicinal. He thought of a gin and tonic: clear and intoxicating at the same time. A few minutes of silent walking brought them to an opening from which they could see the river, the cliffs of the shore on the other side, and also upstream, the nearest peaks of snow-capped mountains. It felt again almost too big to Grady. He'd grown up in a smoggy town on the East Coast and was unused to majestic views like this. It was almost as if his senses, having allowed these sights in, then rejected them as any sort of reality.

They stood not saying anything for a while, beyond the initial Wow they'd both uttered, almost involuntarily.

If we go down there a bit, Shelly said finally, there's another good view.

But there's no path.

I know. It's kind of a secret. Come on.

She stepped out of the clearing in her tennis shoes, and picked her way over logs and moss-covered rocks so nimbly that she was soon out of Grady's sight. He tried to keep an eye on her through the thick growths of ferns. He knew her general location, but he needed to devote the greater part of his attention to where he placed his own feet. Rivulets and unexpected slick spots caused him more than once to have to brace himself.

Over here, Shelly called from a glade to the side of where he stood. He clambered over and was abruptly presented with another panorama, this one opening downstream. The thundering river and the other shore—massive tilting slopes and broad blocks of land imposed on him the feeling of being very small. He recalled the connection between panic and the name of the Greek nature god, thinking this might be a good moment for an antidotal meditation practice, if he could think of one. The only thing that came to him was to relax. Accordingly, he tried to soften his gaze, to open out his hearing, and to simply be there. He knew from things he'd read that he should try to just let this in, if possible, dissolve his boundaries.

After some time of this Shelly stepped in front of him and turned to face the river. She took his hands, encircled herself with them, and placed them on her breasts. Shortly she began—subtly at first and then explicitly—to rub against him. Grady's gauzy awareness vanished. He felt instead the unmistakable, localized gathering of energy, and despite fatigue, as the embrace went on, he asked, into her ear, Now? Right here?

Over there, she said, pointing with her head. Where I can put my hands on that branch.

The place sold no cocktails during cocktail hour, though both Oregonian beer and wine were available. Grady saw that a group

surrounded Lars; they stayed fastened to him through a steady
stream of his anecdotes, and with the active way he listened to
theirs. He leaned forward, roared at jokes, raised his considerable
eyebrows at concerns. Pipe smoke surrounded Lars and rose in
a cloud above him. The young woman selling the drinks looked
at it askance from time to time, but there was nothing she could
do: smoking indoors wasn't illegal in this state, though legislation
was pending. Even if it had been forbidden, Lars possessed such
obvious charisma he probably would have been exempted.

A trim young man, clean-shaven, with hair fashionably cut,
approached Grady to introduce himself. He explained that he'd
arrived with his boyfriend—who had not been expected—and
that they'd managed to book one of the private double rooms;
he wouldn't be in the room with Grady after all. The exchange,
like the person, was short, informative, and pleasant. It lasted less
than three minutes.

No sooner had the young man rejoined his friend and gone
off to other parts of the group than Shelly came over to ask, What
did *he* want?

He told me—

Do you know who that is?

Well, he just told me his name—

That's Benjamin Jay Burgess. He's very hot right now, very
much in demand, especially with ad agencies. I just heard he'll be
doing some titling work for Disney.

Isn't that good?

Yes, but he's eating everyone else's lunch. There isn't so much
work around, you know.

Grady hadn't known. He hadn't thought about it.

I'm not saying he's not good—he's *very* good. His classical alphabets are perfect and his feeling for when and how to ornament them is amazing. It's just that somehow it doesn't feel fair. He kind of comes out of nowhere, just appears, and suddenly he's the darling of art directors. They're shuffling a lot of work his way right now. You see his letters everywhere.

He just appeared? I mean—

Well, he took some classes from Andrea, and then he was in L.A. for a while, studied with Wally... She rattled off a few names that meant nothing to Grady. Andrea feels mixed about him, but she's kind of proud.

All he said to me was that he came here with his boyfriend, they managed to get a double, and so he wouldn't be in the room. Seemed nice enough.

Oh, he's *very* nice, Shelly said, practically spitting out the words. She handed Grady her wine glass. Can you get me another of these, please? I have to go to the room for a minute. Red.

Grady had found no opening to speak with Lars at the cocktail hour, so it was an uplifting surprise when Lars, and some people accompanying him, stopped at Grady's seat on the way up to the speaker's chair after dinner. Grady stood to greet him, shook Lars's hand, and leaned in close to make sure he could hear in the chatter. Would it be OK if I said tonight that you knew how to do Zen meditation? Lars asked.

Me?

Yes. I think it might fit with what I want to talk about.

OK.

Good. Good, Lars said, pressing Grady's hand. Thank you.

Most in the room—between fifty and sixty listeners this evening—were to some degree familiar with Lars's work. They'd either studied with him in college or read one of his instruction manuals, heard him speak at promotional events, or seen one of the many articles he'd published. He'd acquired a certain fame, teaching what he saw as the essential virtues of Italic handwriting, and arguing for its place in the schools. He thought the handwriting young people currently learned, based on a copperplate script, tended to a rapid degeneration of letterforms.

Before his calligraphy courses became popular, Lars had taught a broader swath of art history, and before that, he'd lectured in English literature. The books in his personal library, into which Grady and many others had been invited for seminars, bristled with notepapers and were covered in handwritten marginalia. The texts appeared to be, for Lars, not so much repositories of knowledge as living conversations. He'd read art history and literature from Asia as well, and through this, and through personal contact with craftspeople up and down America's West Coast, he had a working knowledge of these traditions.

Lars held all this learning loosely, but near, and he gave talks of surprising synthetic variety. He had his touchstones. It would not startle most of his listeners, for example, if he landed on the importance of calligraphy in the practice of haiku poetry. They might not know ahead of time how he would get there, or where he might go next, but whichever way it would be, he would generally drive home his points with great effect. If you didn't want to go under Lars's spell, if you didn't want to accept his ideas, even temporarily, you were better off not attending his talks.

This group specifically did want that. They'd paid money and traveled for the privilege. Thus it was an uncomfortable moment for Grady when Lars turned toward him and announced that Grady Ray had agreed tonight to come up and show you all how to do Zen meditation. Isn't that right? Can you come up now, Grady?

Though Grady had been caught off guard by the request and did not want to draw time or attention away from Lars, it was a command, a public one. Lars's eyes were sparkling in a smile behind his thick lenses, and there was no escape. It was also something Grady knew how to do, from his life at the center. He'd gone through the primary technique dozens of times for visitors. His presentations there were usually bare-bones, as free from personal comment or opinion as possible. He'd take questions at the end, but only a couple. Tonight he could be even briefer, he hoped, since everyone was on chairs and thus there was no need to demonstrate the various styles of seating oneself on a pillow and crossing one's legs, topics of hot interest back at the center. Tonight he thought he could get away with just describing things from the hips up.

As Grady went through the instructions for the body, Lars, distractingly, did his best to arrange himself in meditation posture as well, even putting aside his pipe. Other audience members did the same. When Grady saw that everyone was set, when he'd explained how to follow the breath, and how to work with the inevitable onslaught of thoughts, he heard Lars whisper, Ten minutes.

We'll try this for a few minutes, Grady told the group, realizing that he wore no watch, nor had he any bell or gong with which to begin or end the sitting. He scanned the postures in the group for the first couple of minutes, then retracted the sphere of his attention until he himself was in a proper frame of mind. His breath began to slow, and he felt the smack on the back of the head he'd gotten in the parking lot. His thighs and his limbs generally were leaden, probably, he surmised, from exertions with Shelly. A cascade of images and confused feelings connected to this also appeared.

Soon Grady had to force his eyes wide open and blink to clear them. He knew this would only give him a couple of minutes of wakefulness, but he thought it might be enough. Despite verging on sleep in front of a large audience, he understood the obstacles he was facing: there had been two beers before dinner, a generous helping of potatoes and gravy at the meal itself, a piece of cream pie after, the warmth of the fire behind him, the closeness of the room… He saw among members of the audience that he was not alone in feeling the effects of a travel day. From Lars, off to his left, he heard the rasp of a smoker's breath and an occasional glottal catch, perhaps the beginning of a snore.

Grady cleared his own throat and said, in what he hoped was a soothing tone, When you finish a period of mediation, it's good to move very gently at first. Then he talked about testing feet and legs before putting weight on them. As he spoke, he wondered how long they'd sat—had they done ten minutes? Lars seemed pleased enough.

I was thinking, Lars told the group, that we could have a period of meditation before breakfast each morning. What time would you like to start, Grady? Six-thirty? Seven? We can meet right in here. Lars swept his arm around the room, from the stone fireplace behind him to the circular arrangement of audience chairs. This being the first Grady had heard of the plan, he chose the later time and said so as he slipped back to his seat. He could see Andrea, beaming approval at him from her place. Slowed by the short sitting period, Lars wound his talk to a close earlier, perhaps, than he otherwise might have done, and not without the tacit agreement of the group.

Shelly and Grady walked out together. She'd come over to tell him the meditation instruction had been nice.

You're alone in your room, did you say?

Seems yeah.

So are you up for a visit later?

He turned to look at her and they both smiled. I wouldn't say no, he teased, but I do have to get up.

I heard. I'm not talking about all night. We were two in a single bed *last* night, remember? I'm tired too.

Grady had no awareness of falling asleep, but Shelly's knock woke him. She let herself in. Though he was stiff and sore, and disoriented from being awakened, his body responded with surprising quickness to Shelly. They put on the lamp by the empty bed and found it acceptably low. Candles, incense, cigarettes—any fire was forbidden in the rooms. But they both, it turned out, wanted some light: they enjoyed looking at each other and found it exciting to watch their intercourse. At some point, Grady swiveled his travel alarm clock to the wall so he wouldn't think about it.

When it rang, he found himself alone in bed. He dragged himself up, washed quickly, dressed, and made his bleary way along several corridors to the central area. There he found a table with a Samovar on it, beside rows of different teas, instant coffee, powdered milk, and cups. Ignoring the magic marker and roll of masking tape by the cups, he took one and made instant coffee in it. Labeling a cup for personal use, as he knew he was meant to do, would be a bigger design challenge at a convention of calligraphers than at other gatherings. He'd deal with it later. The important point was to get caffeinated.

The area Lars had indicated for meditation, when empty, was basically a rectangular section of carpet in front of an enormous stone fireplace. There were couches bordering the carpet, and clusters of folding chairs on it, in the disarray they'd taken after Lars's talk. A fire had backed Lars as he spoke; this morning, ash and unburnt ends of wood lay in the hearth. A small draft blew through the fireplace occasionally, raising minuscule puffs of ash. Was it true, Grady wondered, that the word *nirvana* originated in the picture of a fire gone out, extinguished, cooled? If so, it looked this morning like a forlorn goal.

People began to drift in, and they helped Grady arrange the sitting area. He'd sit in front, and there'd be rows of chairs, maybe two, staggered so they were not directly behind one another. A pair of older women came in wearing tights and carrying blankets. They asked if they could use them as cushions, to sit on the rug. It was a good idea, and Grady wished he'd thought of it.

As they were ready to begin, Lars shuffled in, attended by the same two women who'd been with him the night before. Grady didn't know if one of them might be Lars's second wife or not. Lars went through a series of attempts to clear his throat, which led to spasmodic coughing, which led to a couple of explosions on the level of a sneeze. If these hadn't been helpless bodily reactions, one would have to think of them as yelling. Eventually the noise subsided. Grady reviewed the instructions briefly and commenced the sitting period. He badly missed having a gong, but after several minutes, a sort of calm blanketed the group anyway. They were twelve, he saw, including himself.

A certain amount of banging and loud talk emanated from the kitchen, with the cooks loudly shushing one another as they went along the back wall to the breakfast buffet. Grady could see, though the others could not, that a group of people was forming in one of the hallways, trying to decide if they could approach the coffee area. The cooks moving back and forth emboldened first one, then more of the participants, who made their way to the station, mixed a hot drink, and went off. Some stood raising and lowering tea bags in their cups absentmindedly, looking over at the sitters. Being observed in this way contributed to the self-consciousness Grady already felt sitting in front.

The breakfast setup and hot-drink traffic accompanied them for their half-hour sit, preventing—certainly on Grady's part—anything like absorption. Back at the center, official word was that if you showed up and tried sincerely to do the technique, one meditation session was as good as another. It was a theological point of some importance: meditation was not to be judged or graded. It didn't always feel that way, though. Without a bell, Grady spent the latter part of this period wondering how he could best end it. He couldn't borrow from the Quakers the pleasant gesture of turning to a neighbor and shaking hands. The first row was beyond his reach, and he certainly didn't want to shock anyone by rising without warning and approaching them with an outstretched arm. He finally decided on a stage clearing of his throat, then placing his hands palm to palm in front of his chest and bending forward in a bow. Surprisingly many in the group returned his bow, as if they'd been doing it for years.

Grady took a gentle, full-body bump from Shelly as he stood in the breakfast line. He returned it, and smiled as he let her cut in, before helping himself to the bacon they never got at the center and the French toast, which appeared there only rarely. He told Shelly meditation had been fine, and that, yes, Lars had shown up. One of the two women at Lars's side had indeed been his new wife, he learned—the one with the highlights in her hair. Grady confessed that he hadn't noticed the highlights. Shelly went on to say she meant the younger one, and to gesture with her hands as to the woman's physical stature. The other one was apparently her sister.

Lethargy weighed on his eyes as Grady seated himself and began ordering his work. He felt the tiredness in his arms as well, which meant it might affect his writing. Understanding this to be the inevitable dip after a large breakfast, he wondered if another coffee might help. At the center, during days of extended sitting, he had only to consider his bladder. Here, he was more concerned with the shakes that had lately begun to creep into his hand.

He first measured and ruled out guidelines on the next sheet of his manuscript. Such tasks were rote, but sufficiently exacting as to help him enter a calligraphic state of mind. The lines within which he would write needed to be clear to his eye—but only just. He drew them with a hard pencil, trying to keep the pressure on the paper even and light all the way across. Twelve lines of text meant a lot of guidelines. He'd experimented in the past with scoring the paper invisibly, using an edged bone fold to impress the lines. The parallel furrows had reflected light from certain angles, but it turned out to cause Grady eyestrain. Additionally, the grooves in the surface of the paper could unexpectedly draw ink into them, or catch a corner of his nib.

When he'd first seen medieval manuscripts he'd noticed that the scribes—if indeed it had been the scribes who'd done it—used a variety of solutions for guidelines. In some cases, they'd made the lines red or green or blue, using them as design elements instead of hiding them. Grady didn't really see guidelines anyway when looking at a page of writing, unless they were obnoxiously thick or dark. The letters themselves moved his eye along.

He ruled both sides of the sheet without mishap, sprinkled it lightly with a grease-absorbent powder, and nestled it in a pad of paper he used for storage. From the same pad he extracted his current sheet, as well as a protective page, to cover all but the line he was actually writing. He also pulled out an old sheet of misruled paper and began to do his warm-ups on it.

He did these things, but it all felt like a struggle. Nothing was where it should be: the angle of the lamp and the light it cast was wrong; the reach to his ink too far; his blotting sheet wasn't where it should be. His ability to spread out was cramped by other calligraphers, and because his project was a sacred text, he couldn't simply set things on the floor.

Part of this rising irritation was simply that he was restarting a delicate task. Probably watchmakers went through this at the beginning of a workday; maybe diamond cutters back from holiday had to submit to similar barriers around the still space of their tiny chisel and big lens. Grady knew at least that nothing could be rushed. Whenever he had to, as at the center sometimes, results were variable.

There, word of a newly deceased person might be given to him at the start of a meditation period, with the understanding that he should leave the hall and go prepare a memorial card of sufficient size and dignity in time for the services. He usually had about half an hour. Being in his own workspace, and the fact he'd been in meditation, usually helped him. But there was never time for rewriting. If a letter looked bad, or if the spacing was off, so it would remain. The card would sit on the main shrine at least three days, where he would have to look at it, especially if he was assisting in the ritual.

At this retreat there was no time pressure, though the thin concentration he had developed would last only so long. He was tired, and there was a great deal else going on; primarily, there were dozens of other calligraphers in the room. They were all applying themselves to roughly the same tasks Grady was, but they were all different. Everyone had their own ways of warming up, and distinct rhythms at which they worked. In the intervals when he looked up from his paper—to rest his eyes, or to uncramp a shoulder or a finger, or increasingly, to yawn—Grady found it fascinating to watch other people. Far easier, in fact, than returning his attention to the lettering on his own table—at the moment, the word *illuminating*. All those parallel lines and connecting arches—a word like this, a combination of letters like this, invited misspellings, particularly if he didn't get through it in one go.

In this discipline of black and white, the possibility of mistakes was very real. Wrong definitely existed. There was no shrugging away a misspelled word. It brought things to an unpleasant halt, the way a pedestrian, talking to a friend, might encounter an iron streetlamp in mid-step. Grady did not require of himself the ritual bath and associated prayers Hebrew scribes did whenever they miswrote something in a Torah, but he was stopped by a mistake. He wasn't sure if Buddhist tradition required similar purifications—he wasn't even sure whom to ask, and he hesitated to increase the pressure on an already difficult act. But there were practical decisions: discard the page entirely, and start over? Try to transform the offending letter? Get out a sharp blade and hope the paper would support scraping?

Thus, when on the descending loop of a *g* he realized upon coming back that he'd fallen very briefly asleep—or been gone some way from his work—he put his pen down. The glories of the scriptorium will be few this morning, he thought, as he minimally cleaned his instrument. He covered his paper with another piece of fabric. As unobtrusively as he could, he rose from his place. He tried hard to create no distraction, to draw no attention his way, not even by letting something as incorporeal as his gaze get around. He did not need to know what Shelly or Andrea were doing; he did not want to engage Lars; he did not look around in the slightest. He needed a nap.

Apart from profound disorientation upon waking up an hour before lunch, Grady was able to look back at his day with some satisfaction. He'd showered, straightened and aired the room, managed some progress on his manuscript in the afternoon. Shelly had guided him—innocently this time—along other trails when they both cut out of the cocktail hour, and Lars had neither alluded to meditation nor called on Grady to speak during the fireside chat. Lars had announced a different room for the next morning's meditation. Despite every appearance of dozing through it all, he told Grady he too had found the breakfast setup a noisy background.

Better rested than the previous evening, Grady was able to rise and open the door to Shelly's quiet knock. They embraced as soon as the door closed. Soon they were both naked, and loosely entwined. Grady marveled at her inventiveness; nothing seemed routine or repetitive in her lovemaking. The ways she arranged her body with his, the things she thought of doing—wanted to do, and to have done to her—and all that she said as they engaged in it thrilled him. She was sexually hungry and somewhat crude. Grady had labored through the afternoon in stillness, writing ancient sacred words, and her energy hit him where he needed it. She literally hit him too, in a continuation of the slaps and open-palm punches she'd loosed the nights before. These didn't seem particularly calculated to Grady as he received them. He thought they might be uncontrolled surges of energy, currents of power running through her limbs, so that when they reached the extremity they caused her to flail. He began to return them to the fleshier parts of her otherwise thin body. When he needed a break from genital stimulation, he separated himself and methodically beat the backs of her thighs and her ass until she was reddened with his handprints. Is that all you've got? she asked, looking back over her shoulder at him.

Grady understood that if he wanted to see her back home, he would have to find out about Waverly—Waverly and whoever else. He wasn't even sure where she lived. His own life was uncomplicated in this regard at present, though complex in other ways. He'd told her little about himself so far, and he knew little about her. *Graphic artist, calligrapher, likes hiking and nature and*

Spanish food: so might read a description if he were composing one for a listing. He probably could put in more than *lithe, athletic, creative.* He would have to forgo descriptions of her coppery skin, her dark-red nipples, her peppery taste; he could mention the green eyes, but maybe not her thick lips—lips that encircled him now, he saw, as he snapped free from thoughts. With her hands free, she reached around and slapped his buttocks hard, and again. *Likes spanking,* he added.

They were horrified to hear, as they lay together during a pause, chairs or other furniture being moved around in a neighboring room. Were the walls really so thin? Had they been loud? Their eyes met to exchange this thought, but then the gaze continued. Instead of speaking, Grady slid closer and soon they were kissing again.

I think they're moving the beds together, Shelly said.

You think?

I'd like to think so.

Loud or not, the newly permitted smacking aspect of their sex made it go on much longer. Even though they hadn't been keeping track of time before, Grady knew that tonight they were doing more. How could they not? They'd entered a realm of intoxication, a rare space in which they were mutually drunk on sexual energy, vaulted by the connection of their bodies into a god realm, a way of being that ran on bliss, and was oblivious to limits of the clock, or even to the bodies they'd used to arrive in it. It felt to Grady as sublime as any absorption he'd ever experienced, including the making of art, or the ones described in the meditation texts he wrote out. He knew that he'd only had the tiniest tastes of these— the classical spiritual states, the samadhis—but who was going to tell him, especially now, that what he was feeling was inferior? This was heaven; this did not come along every day; this was literally fucking amazing. Praise the gods.

The problem with the god-states, he reflected next morning, is that they don't last. The conditions that give rise to them come to an end, and the fall from grace isn't pleasant. At least this was what the tradition said, and so it seemed to Grady too as he rose and tried to prepare himself to lead meditation. The texts mention how a pungent smell might presage a god's fall; he could not but wonder about this as he tried to wash off—from his hands and face, at least—the layers of sweat and other dried fluids they'd been covered in. Perceptions generally felt harsh this morning: light in the bathroom, too dim to be useful for shaving, was certainly bright enough to force his eyes into a squint; air that rolled into the room when he opened a window brought with it not only perfume from the trees and shrubs, but a damp chill; the abrasive note his alarm clock forced at him had been only the first sound to annoy. Now everything—from the drip in the sink to the click of the door— seemed to have a mocking edge, to be dragging his mind toward a dull space that wished only to be undisturbed.

He knew these signs to be just that—messages to repair this fatigue. The center put on marathon meditation sessions several times each year, and in the course of these Grady had gone through similar hard-edged feelings of exhaustion. He knew not to fight with them, or to give in to despair; they would change. If it felt like hell now, only recently it had been heaven. Residents in both realms, however, were cursed with thinking their stays would be endless.

He went out the fire door instead of winding his way through the hallways. His intention was to circle the building in open air and get to the meditation space at least a little refreshed. He arrived on time, bearing a cup of coffee, which he consumed as they set up. They opted for a circle this morning, reflecting the shape of the room, but ended up with a semicircle, Grady's seat facing the others. It reminded him of diagrams of how lenses focus light. His seat would be at the place where the beams converged—a kind of hot spot. Back at the center, with very rare exceptions, everyone sat close to and facing a wall, though this tradition varied from school to school. He had done retreats where meditators sat facing the center of the room—facing out, people said—though they sat well back from one another in straight lines.

The group this morning used a mixture of chairs, cushions. and folded blankets again, and Grady was touched when the two ladies from yesterday offered him a blanket. One of them also extended a leotard-covered arm to hand over a set of finger cymbals. She'd brought them, she whispered, so that she could practice her belly dancing during breaks. I have to *move* sometimes! she said. Grady nodded in agreement and thanks.

When everyone had settled—including Lars, his wife, and her sister—Grady struck the cymbals together three times. By comparison with the bowl-shaped Japanese gongs he was used to, these high-pitched tings gave him the feeling of calling to order an assembly of air-sprites and fairies. In fact, there were again twelve or thirteen people, a slightly different composition from the day before. He was pleased to see Andrea there, though she too began the period with a round of deep coughing, echoing Lars's. Eventually the room quieted. For ventilation, Grady had left the sliding door slightly ajar, but they were mostly cut off from outside noises. This had the effect of magnifying sounds within the room.

Having slept again only little, Grady had slim hope of being able to stay awake for the entire meditation. After perhaps a ten-minute ride on the coffee, he felt pretty sure that following his breath would lead him to sleep. Still, he assumed the meditation posture as best he could, and at least tried in his drowsy state not to rock like a metronome in front of the group. It was a defensive practice, he knew, warding off what was actually happening. But people were facing him; he felt them looking. It seemed necessary to stay awake, just as it did at the center, where hall monitors patrolled the room, bearing their flat sticks and ritually whacking sleepy meditators.

Again, stillness descended on the group, and Grady felt his own attention to his breathing fade as the rhythm of it grew more subtle. He knew that to try to follow his breath would be to stir it up unnecessarily. The trick now was in how to stay alert without getting on any particular train of thought for very long, and without trying to deepen, or heighten, anything. Classical instructions at this point were generally negatives: don't do this, don't do that, don't even try to meditate. Those teachers hadn't sat in a small room with Lars, thought Grady, because if anything was impossible to ignore, it was Lars—primarily his heavy breathing, but his body too. Perhaps it came from years in front of a classroom or a lecture hall: willing attention his way. Whatever the cause, his body took up space powerfully. It was like sitting in the room with a bear: Grady saw meditator, meditator, meditator, grizzly bear, meditator...

And Lars was loud. Constant smoking had made every aspect of his breath audible. It wasn't as long, or as slow, or as crucial, as the breath of someone dying, but it felt hypnotic. Grady finally gave up resisting. I've followed his mind for years, watched it move in his talks; I've followed his hand across pages large and small as it wrote. Why shouldn't I spend the next quarter hour following his breath? Do I have something better to do?

For Grady, the conference ran to conclusion with two more days patterned the same way: early meditation, a midmorning nap, some progress on his manuscript in the afternoon, a nature walk with Shelly at the cocktail hour, Lars's talk after dinner, and some hours coupling with Shelly at night. She seemed better suited to this schedule than he was; she made it through the morning work session, only taking a nap after lunch, when her roommates enforced a kind of quiet time in their dorm.

Andrea caused general delight on one of the evenings by explaining, at Lars's request, how she'd had to rework a T-shirt design. In a solemn Fraktur, she'd written *The pen is mightier than the sword*—a sentiment widely shared by the group. She showed her mock-up: there, she'd begun the sentence with a curvy, swashbuckling T and had isolated *mightier* on a line by itself. On a T-shirt, this would run across the breast. The problem had come at the printer's, when the man in his apron had questioned her first line: two words or three? If she'd meant two words, he wasn't going to print that, he told her. He could give her the name of another shop that dealt in such work, but not his place. Only then had Andrea seen that she needed more space between the second and third words.

She had to rewrite the first line, and then it looked oddly grafted to the other two, so that she then had to rewrite the whole thing. Several times. Andrea told the story well: each setback brought more laughter. Events that no doubt caused hot embarrassment at the time now brought only merriment. Instead of the string of curses she'd surely let loose—Andrea was a cultivated, subtle person, but she could swear shockingly— amusement filled the air. At the end of her talk, she did a brisk business with the shirts.

Grady stood back to be last in line. After paying for a T-shirt, he made arrangements with Andrea for the next day. He would ride in the car as far as the Portland airport and disembark there. Andrea agreed to taking his materials back down to the Bay Area and storing them in her overcrowded studio, where he'd collect them upon return. Grady said he'd travel to Boulder, spend a few days there, then continue on to Ohio for a brief family visit. He thought he'd be back in about ten days.

We'll miss you, she said, packing up the shirts. I guess the car will be…lonelier on the ride back. That she held his eye for a fraction of a second caused Grady to wonder if she was referring to Shelly and him. They had been mostly discreet at the retreat, though they'd also let themselves be seen together in public sometimes. And there were the thin walls. Shelly, of course, might have been talking to Andrea directly; Andrea often formed close relationships with her students. Grady wondered briefly if there were a female version of the word *avuncular*, but he couldn't think of it, if it existed. On the other hand, he *could* think of several times through the years he'd confided things to Andrea.

Maybe it'll be lonely on the plane ride too, he offered.

I doubt that, she said. Give my love to Bridget if you see her. She paused, then named another two of her students who'd migrated from California to Boulder, part of an exodus provoked by recent earthquakes on the West Coast, and the attractions of a spiritual, artistic, and literary community growing around a Buddhist teacher in the Rockies. It was referred to as "the scene" and it was indeed what Grady wanted to go have a look at.

He thought, as he made his way back to his room, that he and Shelly had also been discreet between themselves. They'd explored each other's bodies thoroughly, and he hoped to continue that tonight—but they'd also kept things back. It would be hard to say what, exactly. Being with Shelly reminded Grady of his earliest sexual encounters—with friends, if he was honest, and in one dim memory, with a cousin. These had felt like going on adventures together, or playing games. He and his cousin had in fact played a formal game, exchanging roles as doctor and patient to examine each other—first through, then under, their pajamas. Now you check my heartbeat. Put your hand here, she'd said, unbuttoning her flannel pajama top, causing the fragrance of her warm skin to pour out at him, overwhelming. He'd always liked that cousin; he liked her to this day. Similarly, a cloud of benevolence surrounded his relations with Shelly, despite their limited time, and a curious biographical reserve. Maybe this was what making love pointed to: that by entwining bodies, putting them next to, on top of, inside of each other, they were manufacturing good feeling? Something beyond orgasms.

They did go together well: they were considerate with each other and also sometimes selfish, in ways they both found exciting. But their motions were not quite affectionate or tender. It sometimes seemed to Grady they verged on performing, rather than expressing anything. Not that he minded much. He was surprised he noticed at all, given the appetites that had pushed him around most of his adult life. It felt odd to him that he should now be making such a distinction. Maybe he just needed a break. He was sore; that was true. They'd abraded each other with their passions. But this was the last night of the conference and he was grateful she would come see him again. He was counting on it.

Shelly had given Grady a business card and a flyer so that they could, possibly, continue their connection back in the Bay Area. There had been no promise. They hadn't known each other before the conference; their paths hadn't crossed. Now they had.

The first obstacle Grady faced was that he didn't own a car. He drove, of course, and sometimes he did business in one of the center's vehicles. If he planned well, he could borrow a car when he needed to, especially if he returned it with more gasoline than when he took it. But it took work. Shelly lived in Marin County; her card listed only a P.O. box, though she'd written a street address and some directions in the margins of the flyer.

It turned out not to be completely rural when he found it one afternoon: there were other houses on the street, but not many, and there was no curb or sidewalk. He parked behind a car in the driveway to avoid blocking the narrow road. Her greeting at the door had been friendly, but with what seemed to be a businesslike edge. After all, he'd arrived—she'd allowed him to come—during her work time. He thought later that he'd also experienced the brief house tour differently than she'd intended it: she was showing him physical space; he felt he was being introduced to a person.

Least startling was the front room. He'd seen the workspace she'd constructed in Oregon, and he'd visited a number of other local calligraphy studios. Writing boards, bottles of ink and other dark liquids, jars full of quills and pens, a careful arrangement of light, the fact that she still wore an ink-stained apron as she pointed around the room—none of this surprised him. A pin-board along one wall, the books on her shelves—all familiar. He took it in from the door. The room across the hall was her son's room, she said.

Ah.

He was at school for another couple of hours, she said. She'd have to go get him.

Mmm. How old was he?

He was eight.

Jason's father lived in Menlo Park, it turned out, where he designed and developed type for computer screens.

Um-hmm.

There was a bathroom at the end of the hall. The big room on the other side of the house held a television, couch, and recliner at one end, and at the other, closer to the kitchen, a small dining table with four chairs. On a sideboard stood a picture in a frame.

Your folks?

Yeah, they're in Chicago.

Another picture, magnetized to the refrigerator, showed these same two people with a young boy against a background of trees.

That's from a year ago, she said. Golden Gate Park. Jason's six there. They came out for his birthday.

She sat Grady in a breakfast nook in the kitchen, and gave him a coffee. Then she set down a plate of cookies, and took one herself.

Where's your room? Where do you sleep?

Back there. I'll show you. But let's have coffee first; I'm really tired.

So they caught up: his trip East, her ride back down from Portland. Did she know Andrea's students in Boulder? One, not the others, though she was familiar with their work—it had been in store windows all up and down Telegraph Avenue, and some was still there, cut into wood and hung out as shingles. Shelly explained how on the long drive back Andrea had brooded about Lars's decline. She feared he didn't have long.

As they talked, as he listened to her and drank her strong coffee, Grady had an unbidden vision of Shelly amid the strands of her life: some she held in her hands; others tangled around her ankles or reached for her neck and hair. There were many more than he'd thought about. Here he sat in her kitchen, eating her cookies, drinking her coffee, taking up the time she needed to make her living.

This is my room, she said, stopping inside the door of it so abruptly that Grady nearly bumped into her. He took advantage of this to wrap her in his arms, which she allowed, but did not at first respond to.

Lots of closet space behind those, she said, pointing to the panels of mirrors along one wall. But not many windows. She nodded to a couple of them, cut high in the wall, curtained off.

I don't spend much time in here during the day, anyway.

Then she swiveled to him, returned his embrace, and kissed him on the mouth. Soon they migrated to the bed, and shortly they were out of their clothes.

Driving home, especially sitting in the heavy traffic that began miles before the bridge, Grady found himself thinking about Shelly in ways that had become familiar to him in approaching classic Zen stories, the koans. He'd never felt he was much good at practicing with those; but through the years, working with a series of teachers, he had heard these cryptic tales expounded in different styles. The cases sometimes began with a verse added by a commentator; sometimes they just opened with description of an encounter—between monks, usually—that seemed to make little sense on a rational level. Students were told by current teachers that all the characters in the stories, the authors of the verses, and even the anthologizer of the collections, were deeply enlightened Zen meditators, and that contemplation of the texts would yield benefit. The collections were thought of as lineage treasures; study of them was urged on modern practitioners, sometimes very forcefully. The how of the study was less clear. Basically, you were supposed to grapple with them any way you could.

Sometimes engagement took place during gatherings for formal meditation. Ideally, it was supposed to expand from there into daily life—as background, or as a subconscious stream of contemplation that might from time to time emerge into view. Such answers as appeared were to be presented to the teacher privately, maybe in terms similar to the case itself—a gesture, or citation. If you tried responding with everyday speech, it would best be non-discursive, or at least surprising. Traditionally, answers were rejected quickly, often cut off mid-presentation. The encounters were understood as bouts in an intense, personal, spiritual wrestling match that could continue for years. Cases and the characters in them frequently formed the core of a teacher's talks to the assembly.

Grady recognized that he was not at present in meditation, though his car, and many hundreds of others around his, sat rumbling, more or less still. Nor was Shelly any kind of monk—she'd shown no interest in meditation, and she hadn't come to even one of the sittings. But she *had* engaged the time and energies of this serious Zen student, and she had effectively thrown his life into puzzlement. Grady was not hoping for enlightenment, whatever that might be, as he turned things around in his mind. He'd just be grateful for insight as to where he fit into her life—relative to Waverly, for example—or where Shelly might fit into his. He also understood that there were differences between entering the story of long-ago monks from another culture and sliding into an erotic reverie about a woman he'd just left, someone whose scent was literally still on him. There was no teacher sitting knee to knee with him just now, holding a short stick to encourage presentation of an answer. But there *had* been an encounter; the words she'd said had been both ordinary and mysterious, and they occupied his mind. It occurred to him again, as a car cut into his lane, that he did not really regard sex as second-class spirituality.

They had uncoupled so as not to slide onto the floor, and with his hands on her hips he'd urged her, very gently, to turn over. She'd crawled up toward the head of the bed and waited for him up there.

OK? he'd said.

Sure, you know I like it from behind.

But the way she'd said it, almost businesslike, almost as if she hadn't really been talking to him, felt suddenly distant. She had gestured vaguely—a backward flip of her hand toward the middle of his body—and she'd sounded rather as if she'd been answering questions at a job interview. He wondered now, an hour and a half later, what she'd really meant.

It excited Grady to hear her say that she wanted something during sex. Anything. Being given verbal invitation or direction aroused him extremely. He felt it stir in him now, in the car, and he tooted the horn briefly, as much in celebration of his blood as in warning to the next driver edging his way toward Grady's lane, pretending not to see him. Excitement had overridden thinking back in the bed too, but his mind now caught on the word "it" in "I like it from behind." Had she meant him—by literal extension, his—when she'd flung her arm back? Or had the coolness in her voice implied a general preference for The Male Organ in this arrangement—his, Waverley's, possibly her ex-husband's? (Grady had known divorced couples to quietly rekindle this part of their relationship, while maintaining their new, separate domestic situations.) Maybe Shelly was just making a statement. What was the phrase? Maybe it was a sex-positive proclamation, with "it" equaling sex? If so, hallelujah.

But it did not help him much toward clarity in relating to her. Nor, obviously, did this line of thought move him in the direction of utmost, right, complete, perfect enlightenment. The best that could be said of it—and this was not nothing—was that it kept him present. It kept him engaged and awake as he jockeyed for position in the diminishing number of lanes to the bridge. It kept him right there.

Made in the USA
Las Vegas, NV
03 February 2022

42898071R00099